Adelle Stripe w... ...*Black Teeth and a Brill... ...tlisted for the Gordon Burn Prize. ...of Authors' K Blundell Trust Award for Fiction. Adelle is the author of three chapbook collections of poetry, the ... *...s of the Land*, was ... writing has appeared in the *Guardian*, *Quietus*, *Penny Dreadful*, *Caught by the River* and *Chiron Review*. A commissioned poem, *The Humber Star*, was performed at John Grant's North Atlantic Flux for Hull City of Culture and was described by the *FT* as a work of 'fantastic depth and poignancy.' She lives in the Calder Valley, West Yorkshire, UK.

www.adellestripe.com

Praise for *Black Teeth and a Brilliant Smile*

'An affectionate, unsentimental debut novel . . . her dialogue snaps and prickles and brings a talented, troubled woman to life . . . she gives an important story a real spark: Dunbar's energy and mischief bubble in the bleakness' *Guardian*

'The writing fresh and impressive. She is the natural inheritor of Nell Dunn, sensibly eschewing symbolism in favour of a grubbier, jagged economy of expression. A quiet precise genius informs every page' *Morning Star*

'Dunbar's story, every bit as gritty and startling as that of her characters, is captured expertly here. This is an extraordinary book made all the more impressive in being the author's debut novel' *Loud & Quiet*

Black Teeth and a Brilliant Smile

Adelle Stripe

FLEET
2017

FLEET

First published in Great Britain in 2017 by Wrecking Ball Press
This paperback edition published in 2017 by Fleet

1 3 5 7 9 10 8 6 4 2

A CIP catalogue record for this book
is available from the British Library.

ISBN 978-0-7088-9895-6

Typeset in Caslon by M Rules
Printed and bound in Great Britain by
Clays Ltd, St Ives plc

Papers used by Fleet are from well-managed forests
and other responsible sources.

Fleet
An imprint of
Little, Brown Book Group
Carmelite House
50 Victoria Embankment
London EC4Y 0DZ

An Hachette UK Company
www.hachette.co.uk

www.littlebrown.co.uk

*This is a work of fiction and is an
alternative version of historic events.*

*It has been manipulated, re-structured and
embellished. Real people rub shoulders with fictional
characters, some utter words from letters and
scripts; others are gleaned from occasional references,
newspaper cuttings, hearsay or fractured memory.*

*It is not the truth and exists purely
within the realm of speculation.*

Prologue

The darkness barely lifted that morning. Black-ink clouds smothered the fading sun that struggled to reach over the moortop. Streetlamps flickered at half past ten, their sodium glow still illuminating the cracked pavements below. It was almost winter solstice.

The precipitation made her headaches worse. And each thudding storm that sluiced on the rooftops compounded pressure in her brain. She listened to the silence before lightning, as birds emptied the sky. Three flashes of white, a crack through the nets, charge and static flushed through her veins. Curtains were drawn around the flat. A flap of plastic, a car exhaust, the roll of a milk bottle, shattering glass – each sound amplified by the pain. Her body, curled in a foetal position, twitched beneath threadbare blankets.

Empty packets of tablets and bottles lined the bedside table and were piled beneath a fringed lamp with a blown bulb that hadn't been replaced. Paracetamol, Codeine, Jellies, Vallies, discarded foils of used Alka Seltzer. Different drugs in combination. Pharmaceuticals couldn't get close. The postman rattled the door. She ignored him and moaned as sickness washed over her.

Outside, the biting wind whipped through ginnels and shook empty branches over Blackshaw Beck. Andrea rolled out of bed, rinsed her face with a cloth in the bathroom sink, and fumbled around in her drawers, spilling odd socks and tights onto the carpet below. Clean pants, white sweater, stonewash jeans, court shoes. A brush through her frizzy Dunbar hair. A glass of water to take the edge off the shakes.

The bedroom floor was covered in remnants of a script that had spilled out from her bag. She trampled across it, kicked the leaves around the floor and paused for a moment to read her words written on foolscap. Lines for a screenplay that had taken three years.

She remembered the nights locked in her room as her kids banged on her door. Her eyes ran over the lines she had thrown out, a mountain of paper in the gold basket tucked beneath her side of the bed. Familiar characters, bile-ridden dialogue, a portrait of difficult lives. The new one was set in the Beacon and told the story of a loan shark and his gang who terrorized the estate. It wasn't made up. She had seen them dragging people out of their houses. It was supposed to be the script that saved her.

Only Oscar had read it. She trusted his opinion.

He had recently written to her, and sent it back by recorded post. It wasn't what I expected, he said. You can do much better than this. The writing is disappointing, your previous work had a unique tone.

There's nothing special about these characters.

The dialogue doesn't sound like yours.

Sorry not to have better news.

Do keep me posted on anything else you are working on.

Thanks a lot, Andrea said.

She dug into her jean pockets for her last flattened Sovereign Black and rolled it between her fingers until the bent end was back into shape. Her cold fingers opened the dusty jewellery box and unearthed an old metal lighter buried beneath costume clip-ons.

Her feet trampled over Oscar's letter and she shook the last dregs of fluid until a flame appeared. Holding the cigarette between her thumb and index finger she took a long draw into her crackling lungs and stared at her reflection in the dresser's mirror.

Read that a hundred times already, she said. Nowt left to say. Don't even like writing. Don't know why I bother ...

She rubbed her forehead and leaned forward, a throbbing pain in her head had kept her up half the night.

Double shift tomorrow, no point complaining, she sighed, and stumbled into the kitchen where empty cereal boxes lined the Formica top. The sink was piled high with two-day old pots. A radio alarm buzzed in the bedroom.

Will you fucking shut up!

Andrea ripped the alarm out of the wall and threw it onto the sheets. On the bedside table she had left a note the previous night but had no recollection of writing it. The biro ran out halfway through, it switched from red to green.

> *Get money for shopping.*
> *Pick up pouch from baccy man.*
> *Catalogue payment.*
> *Presents for kids.*

On the other side of the paper, written in green, was a note-to-self:

> *Bad points: feel very emotional.*
> *Only want to drink.*
> *Can't sleep and eat.*
> *Hate myself and the way I look.*
> *Want to destroy.*
> *No time for anyone.*
> *Not interested in life.*
> *Always tired.*
>
> *Good points: I am trying.*
> *Want to sleep.*
> *Want to eat.*
> *Want to be my normal self.*

Want to leave the drink alone.
Want the kids to be okay.

After leaving the flat, Andrea keeled down the stairwell and headed through the estate towards her sister's house in the mizzle. A wild hunt raged through her head; pounding and rattling with each footstep. Her vision had dimmed and waves of nausea raced through her.

It was hard to distinguish which house was Kathy's through the weaving rain that bounced off the tarmac and spewed into overflowing drains. Pulling her jacket over her head she ran up the garden path as rain seeped through her shoes. The back door was open, and Kathy was sat inside, watching morning television.

It's me, Andrea said. You got any tablets?

She ran straight up the carpeted stairs and into the bathroom, which was decorated with pink and black tiles. Chintz flowers were stencilled on the door.

Kathy's voice boomed behind her.

Bathroom cupboard. Should be some in there. Are you still rough?

Andrea pulled the capsules from silver foil and drank from the tap. She put her forehead beneath it, running cold water over her face and dried her face with a towel.

Bad head. Can't get shut of it. Do you want to come to the pub?

Too much on. Ask Pam. She might. I've to bottom the house today. In a right tip. State of them windows.

Andrea picked up her bag and sat on the edge of the settee.

Look alright to me. Have you picked up your giro yet? It's double week.

Kathy drank from a steaming cup and stared out towards the storm-chewed street.

Quids in, she said. I'm off into town tomorrow, come if you want. Are you sure you're alright? You look dreadful.

Worst one I've had in years, Andrea said, and moved towards the gas fire. Had this buzzing in my ears for about three days. On top of the migraine. Feel shocking.

You need to get it checked out. I mean it.

It's Christmas. They won't have time to see me.

Andrea pulled the zip up on her jacket, rubbed her palms together and blew on her trembling hands.

Won't even answer the phone when I try and ring. And I'm not traipsing over there; it's about an hour's walk there and back.

How come you went out last night if you were feeling this rough?

Wanted to see Keith. Makes me feel better.

Kathy started to laugh.

Oh, I bet he does.

It's not just about *that*, she replied. If I have a few drinks it goes away. Plus, I like seeing him. Bingley's quiet. Nobody knows me there.

Baking in here, Kathy said. Don't know what's up with you.

I've had the storage heaters on all morning. Even the kids are wearing vests.

Toys were scattered across the rug. Kathy threw them into a box in the corner of the room, and picked up her daughter under one arm. She threw a towel over one shoulder and pushed her face against the baby's nappy.

You need a nappy-change young lady, she said.

Andrea stood up, checked for her keys and made her way out through the kitchen. I'm off for a drink now, she shouted. But I'll be back later, promise.

The water began to soak into the ground as the first rays of sun broke through the clouds, the light reflected off a dented car bonnet. She walked towards the Beacon, her unofficial office on the far side of the Crescent. The only place she could be contacted on the phone. Home from home. Domino games and poker. Slot machines and pool. High enough on the estate to see for miles on a clear day, all the way to Emley Moor Mast. A place to hide and see her mates. Ideas to put down on paper. A pint of lager for less than a quid. Long days that led to oblivion.

Nightly lock-ins in the Tap Room bar. A red Tetley lantern over the door. Old men drunk-walked through the estate with bags full of carry-out before the pub doors opened. Bowland House loomed in the background with boarded up windows and burnt out cars. Stray mutts brawled on the grass. The M62 glowed in the distance.

Andrea sheltered in the corner shop foyer on Reevy Road,

beneath the flaking paintwork and empty crisp packets that chased each other in the breeze. NATIONAL FRONT, a wrong-swastika and AC/DC were sprayed on shop shutters. LUFC and a spunking cock had been scrubbed from the wall, leaving only a faint outline in the morning light. Two teenage girls over the way hung out of their bedroom windows, smoking.

The bar lamps were being switched on in the Beacon and blue icicle fairy lights flashed around the serving hatch. She could see their pulsing light from the roadside. Steps were mottled with old chewing gum, a familiar pattern on the city's streets. She walked up towards the porch, through double doors and turned left. Her watch read 11.55am.

A white plastic fir tree leaned against the bar after being tripped over countless times the night before. Tinsel, cracked baubles and angel's hair were scattered on the floor. Andrea walked around them and made her way towards the Tap Room. Mo, the new landlady, could handle the drinkers, who had already lined up their places at the bar. Sitting in the same places their fathers had sat. And the same places their sons would sit, too. They perched on bar stools and stared in a defeated way at their first pints of the day. The older men whispered in emphysema voices as football clips played on a colour TV. Andrea stood next to them, they were telling dirty jokes already. She felt the pulse race through her throat.

Mo barked at them as they burst out laughing.

Oi, I'll have none of that language! Any more of that and you're out.

Andrea grimaced and ordered half a Castle, her headache engorged since the walk. The air was supposed to do her good. Only alcohol had any effect. She rubbed her furrowed brow, sat in a window seat and waited for the tablets to kick in.

One of the drinkers, Gary, was hunched over the jukebox and selected a rave track. It made a din and was far too early in the day for that sort of noise. He'd been out the night before to the Gallery, and was still grinding his teeth. Beads of sweat formed on his cheeks, and he bobbed his head to the music talking loudly about a man called Luigi. His voice echoed in the bar, booming as he sank his lager.

I swear I saw David Batty in there, he said. And Gary Speed. On one.

Andrea stood up, pulled out change for the machine, and flipped through the compilations behind the glass. Her face squinted at the songs and she chose 'Room in Your Heart'. It started to play as she fumbled around for more coins.

Paddy, one of her father's friends stood behind her and supped on his pint.

Hey, I'm sorry about your fatha. Don't feel right not having him here.

It were for the best, she replied. It were quick. He didn't suffer.

We had some right laughs together. Remember that time we'd been out all day in town, we were legless . . .

Enough. I've got a banging head. Don't want to talk about me Dad. Not today.

She turned her back on him and continued to squint through the screen.

Ooh, seeing your arse today are we?

He pretended to squeeze her backside as she leaned over the coin slot.

No need to be like that just cos you've got an hangover ...

The men at the bar started laughing.

Andrea scowled as she turned her head towards him.

I know what you're doing, she hissed. You must think I was born yesterday.

Paddy slurped the dregs of his pint and rocked from side to side. He winked at her and revealed a mouth of broken teeth.

Smile, it might never happen, he said. Don't you love me anymore?

She could smell the drink on him from the previous day. His shirt was decorated with the remnants of crusted egg and paint. His ginger hair had started balding around the top and his receding hairline glistened off the ceiling's strip-lights.

Andrea swore under her breath and turned her back on him.

He grinned at her and raised his glass as the steam began to rise from the dishwasher. Paddy pulled on the waistband of his tracksuit bottoms and twanged the elastic.

I'll buy you a drink Christmas night. That'll cheer you up.

I won't make Christmas this year, she replied, and walked back to her seat.

In the streets outside sardine-packed buses headed down the hill towards Bradford. The Beacon's windows were clouded with condensation, and water began to drip into the pub from the leaking roof. Mo put a bucket under the leak and emptied the previous night's ashtrays. She noticed Andrea had been sitting in the same position for a while, her back to the rest of the pub, unusual for her.

Mo unloaded clean glasses onto the racks and ate a packet of peanuts by the bar.

Do you think Andrea's alright? she said. She's a bit quiet today.

The drinkers turned around and saw Andrea leaning to one side.

The music continued to bang over the speakers, and Mo turned the volume down. She walked towards Andrea and rested her hand on her shoulder.

Everything okay, love? Do you need some air?

Andrea was crouched over her drink, which she had barely touched. Her head was in her hands. She looked up at Mo with bloodshot eyes. Crimson blotches patterned her face and neck.

Summat wrong. With me face. Feel sick. Me neck's stiff. Can't see properly. Yellow lights. Orange. Red . . .

Here, grab my arm, Mo said. I'll get you some water.

Andrea reached over to Mo as she pulled her up, lurched through the bar and stumbled towards the corridor which led to the toilet and fell through the cream door with a Ladies sign glued to the top her hands out of focus her eyes flickered

11

she retched over the porcelain sink splashing water over her forehead her hair her cheeks her mouth her ears she hung onto the taps rocking backwards forwards and raised her head three of her faces stared back in the mirror's reflection her brain pulsed the heat rose through her skin she slipped she crawled on the floor tiles into the cubicle and was sick in the pan bile and water through her nose her lips the fire rose through her neck and her knees buckled underneath and then everything went black.

Five minutes later Mo walked along the corridor, carrying a pile of freshly laundered hand towels and saw Andrea's legs splayed out on the Ladies' floor. She ran over to her and lifted her head, which was wedged between the door and the painted breeze-block walls.

Andrea, are you there?! she shouted, and put her ear next to Andrea's mouth.

Oh God, she's not breathing . . .

Mo ran to the bar and called 999.

1

Hard Scratch

Mam remembers when the estate was first built. There was nothing here before. Just moors. People took bus tours from all round Bradford to come and see the houses. That's when she first came here with Dad, in the 1950s. Everyone worked at Buttershaw Mills. School said the name means 'in my cottage near a wood' and told us that the streets are built on Millstone Grit, a brown rock that lets water through. Before then everyone lived in the city. The council knocked their houses down after the war. People used to shit in a midden, used ash to cover their muck. Even the kids had to work in the mills. That was a long time ago.

The ground up here is always sodden, and it rains almost every day. Can't wear anything nice. It feels like we're on the edge of everything. Miles to Bradford centre. Miles to Halifax. And we're stuck up here with not much to do. Holme Wood is another big estate. Sometimes I wished I lived there instead.

26 Brafferton Arbor is our home. It's a large house and there are seven of us, plus Mam and Dad. I have three sisters, Pamela, Kathy and Jeanette. My brothers are David, Nigel and Tony. My brother Stephen got run over playing chicken last year. He was eleven. Mam is called Alma and she met Dad in the mills. His name is John Brian. They are from Canterbury estate and got married in 1958; their picture is on our mantelpiece. Dad hasn't changed his hair since then and greases it back in a duck's arse every morning.

After the mills closed Dad worked as a demolition man and had a bad accident so he can't work. A forklift truck almost took his arm off. They lived at a place called Sloan Square in a council flat after they got married, I lived there when I was small but don't remember it much. The council kicked us out because Dad couldn't pay the rent and Mam ended up in a refuge called St. Luke's with all of us. It was horrible and she was pregnant with Jeanette. There was a VD clinic opposite and Mam used to stare out of the window looking at it. Sometimes she cried. In the end the council found us somewhere and that's how we got to Buttershaw. We moved up here just in time for Jeanette to be born in the house.

Some of the flats on Buttershaw have big cracks up the stairwells. My friend Eileen lives in a little flat with six of her brothers and sisters. They sleep three to a bed and some sleep in the living room. The walls are wet inside the flat and when they tried to wallpaper it went black within a week and dropped off. So now they don't bother decorating. Washing gets nicked off the lines and even if they did put

14

it out the weather isn't dry enough, so they hang their washing off the balcony and inside the kitchen. Some other flats have ten people living in them. It has got worse recently. A few houses have broken windows and gardens have mattresses and cookers out the front. The estate has lots of problems but I like it here. It is my home.

It is noisy around Buttershaw, lots of kids. Everyone has big families and some get moved from other parts of Bradford because they cause trouble. On the Crescent police sirens are always going off and in some parts they have grass growing in the gutters. The roofs are all cracked and when I walk past people are always rowing. I sometimes hide in stairwells so I can listen in. The best ones end in a punch-up. The floors are covered in concrete so when they shout it echoes. The lads put their motorbikes out the front and burn old tyres in piles in their gardens.

The old people get cross with the young ones because we don't shut up. They think we make a mess and keep saying they want to leave. But nobody wants to move up here, so some of the old ones are trapped. There's not much for them to do. We don't have a doctor and not many people have cars, so we go on the bus. We have a chippy which is where I go after school. There is a shop called Patel's and they sell newspapers and groceries. We have to go to Great Horton to the supermarket. It's a long way to walk with carrier bags.

Mam went to a meeting to see if we could get better housing for Buttershaw. They send us a newsletter every month and people write letters to complain about dogs and rowdy kids. The council wants money to make our houses better and to put gas fires in. I like sitting round ours on a night, but when it's really cold I sometimes *burn the hairs on my legs and the skin goes pink. Mam says it's dirty having coal and she has to keep cleaning the ornaments because of the soot.*

Outside our house is a patch of grass called the Arbor. It has an old tennis court and hundreds of dandelions. We used to play in it all the time when we were little and even now I go and sit out there with my friends when the sun is out. A tatter put a horse on there and it has a chain to stop it running off. He takes it out scrapping on a cart. It's called Roddy and its nose feels like velvet. It makes my brother sneeze. Some people have pigeons on our street; they keep them in lofts and race them for money. Others have chickens and we get eggs from Mrs Cunningham. The dogs chase them down the road. Our street is always covered in feathers and white dog muck. I am scared of the dogs.

The best thing about living here is that I don't have to go any- where else. There's always things happening and people to talk to. We all look after each other and have a laugh. Every day I go out I hear something that is interesting.

There aren't many other places you could say that about.

*

Along the street living room televisions were being switched on, Andrea walked past the windows peering into people's houses. Doreen and Dick were watching television with trays on their laps, eating their tea in Shackletons chairs. Framed family photographs covered the living room wall. Dick was watching *Love thy Neighbour* and slopped gravy down the front of his jumper as he sniggered at the screen. He always wore a tie and pin underneath.

It was 1975. Andrea was fourteen years old and only had a few pence in her pocket. Eileen joined her that night. They walked around the estate in a circuit, finding out what was going on, and who said what to who. The girls made their own entertainment. If they were lucky they cadged fags from groups of lads who hung around the shop. Sometimes the girls picked on the boys; flirting, teasing, learning how to be a woman. Other nights were spent waiting outside the pub, tagging on to the older men who staggered down the pavements at closing time. One of them was a taxi driver who said he needed babysitters. He thought they were the kind of girls who'd do a good job.

Andrea kept returning to one of the houses on Welbourn Mount. A woman called Judith lived there; it was the cleanest on the street. Each day after dropping her sons off at school, she moved the cupboards, polished windows with vinegar and newspaper and scrubbed the kitchen sink with soda crystals. Andrea watched her from the path outside, moving furniture around in a spotted pinny and wondered what she was doing in there. At dusk Andrea and Eileen waited by the privet hedge to watch her three sons, the eldest of which was their latest crush. The boys went to a different school, St. Bede's.

He's looking good tonight, Eileen said. There he is! He's got his top off. Oh my God. *Phwoaaarrr!*

The front garden was neatly trimmed. Gnomes and plastic birds lined the pathways. The girls could see a Jesus day-glo picture through the window in the front porch and often heard the brass tea trolley rattling against the draft. Over the course of the summer they found out his name from her neighbour, the woman who was always pissed during the day and slept on the deckchair outside, asleep in the midday sun.

The boy was called Craig. Andrea wrote him a teenage love letter that was sprayed with a squirt of Moonwind on the envelope. She pushed it through his letterbox one night, after the lights went out. It was signed with her initials.

After a few weeks of waiting around she noticed he had started to grin back at her through his bedroom window, and watched as she walked past the house. Andrea blushed and walked even faster. She drew his surname in a love heart in the back of her school books. During August each living moment was spent thinking about him; his clothes, his eyes, his laugh, his hair. Time stood still when he asked her on a date. They spent three nights walking through Coley Beck, hiding from the rain under silver birch trees.

When Andrea first noticed her period was late she didn't tell anyone except Eileen. She showed her the blue stick hidden in her top drawer and held it up to the light.

It's my own stupid fault, she said. It takes two to get pregnant. Maybe this was what was meant to happen all along.

Andrea pushed the mustard curtains to one side and leaned

outside. The bedroom was decorated with floral wallpaper and a poster of David Essex was taped to the wall. Old lipsticks, tubs of glitter and discarded piles of school uniform were scattered across the carpet.

Are you sure? Did you do the test right?

Got it from family planning in town. They did one there and then I did it at home again. I'm six weeks late.

Eileen sat on the end of Andrea's single bed and wedged tissue paper between her toes, painting each nail a different colour from the varnish pots on the dresser.

You have to tell Alma, she said. Can't hide it forever.

Andrea rubbed her finger in a pot of rouge and smeared it on her pallid cheeks, rubbing violently until the two waxy marks had covered her face, in large pink rings that looked like a geisha.

It's not Mam that I'm worried about. It's Dad. He's gonna kill me.

Like hell he will. He's a soft sod really.

You don't know what he's like. He wants people to think he's nice but he's a sod really.

She lifted up her shirt, pushed the top of her pants down and pointed to a mark on her hip.

Look at this, I can't tell him who the father is. He'll bray him when he's tanked up.

Don't kill me for saying this, Eileen paused. Have you thought about having an abortion?

Andrea scrunched her face up.

Are you joking?

You could have it over and done with, Eileen said and started blowing on her fingernails. If you wanted I could go with you.

Can't believe you'd even say that. Look, if it's put there, then you *have* to have it. Getting rid of it, that's the easy way out. It's not a punishment you know.

Sorry . . .

Eileen paused and listened to Alma rattling the pots and pans in the kitchen below.

I was just trying to say there's things you can do if you don't want it.

I'm not having an abortion, Andrea replied. And I'm not having it adopted, either.

Well in that case, you have to tell people. Won't be able to hide it for much longer. I can see it poking out when you take your cardie off.

Yeah, I know.

Andrea pulled her cardie around her belly and crossed her arms.

It wasn't meant to be like this, she said.

*

On rainy days, in the darkest months of the year, it sometimes took an hour to travel on the 611 into Bradford. It travelled through Wibsey, past the pubs, and down towards the roundabout at Odsal Stadium. She always sat on the top deck at the front, and rubbed on the mucky glass to see out over Manchester Road. The double-decker was always filled with smoke and seats had foam poking through pen-knife slashes. It stopped at Chester Street, just behind the Alhambra Theatre. The sun broke through the valley from the east on clear days, and she could see Peel Park and Undercliffe peering from the top of the hill. Outside, the air was clogged with diesel fumes and streets were crowded with people criss-crossing towards the market.

That afternoon, she caught the bus with Craig and they walked into the city and around Kirkgate Market, drinking tea in a greasy spoon to shelter from the rain outside.

I've summat to tell you, she said.

Go on.

He pushed a brown piece of lettuce around his plate.

Well, I've been thinking. You know, about the baby.

What about the baby?

I think, after it's born, I might try and get a flat.

On Buttershaw?

Craig brushed his fringe to one side and fiddled with the cuff on his polyester shirt.

Yeah, she said. You could come and help out now and again.

I dunno, he paused. I'm worried. Haven't told Mum yet. She'll be disappointed in me. She allus says I'm like me Dad, you know. Look like him. Act like him. She were pregnant wi me at sixteen. He got her knocked up. Then she were stuck wi him. Until he buggered off and left us.

And? What are you getting at?

It's not too late to give it up. There's loadsa people who want bairns, can't have em. It'd have a good home.

There is no way that's happening . . .

Andrea raised her chin and glowered at him.

I'm keeping it, she said. It might well embarrass you but I don't care what people think. Thought you liked me.

I do, he said.

Craig emptied the teapot's dregs and stared at the residue that clung to the cup.

It's just. Well, the priest said he could help. That there's ways and means . . .

Oh, that's what it's about!

Andrea sniggered at him and picked up her coat from the back of the chair.

Is that what you really think of me? It's *our* baby you know.

Don't be like that. We could still make it work, he said. I promise. We just need to wait a bit. Keep it quiet.

You were meant to be different, she said. More fool me.

Andrea threw her coins onto the table, her face pink from holding back the upset. Her belly was already making her trousers tight. Craig tried to take her hand. She pulled it away. He stood up, brushed his trousers down, and pulled a small box from his pocket and opened it.

22

This was for you. It were only a few quid. But I wanted you to have it.

He put the box into her hand.

I've got my whole life in front of me, he said. So have you. It doesn't have to be like this.

Andrea opened the box and pulled out a small silver ring with a pink rose engraved in the band.

Are you trying to buy me off?

No. It's not about that. It were for you. I picked it from the market. Thought you'd like it.

S'alright I suppose . . .

She turned and started walking through the doorway, and stopped before opening the door. If you don't tell your Mam I certainly will, she said.

So is that it then? Are you calling it a day?

Just about, she said.

He put his wallet into his top pocket, blew his nose into a check handkerchief and lowered his head.

Alright then, Andrea. Guess I'll see you around.

*

Came home from school last night. Mam asked if I was alright. I said yes and ran upstairs. Pam was getting ready to go out. She said look at your gut, have you been on the chips again. I said no and pulled my jumper down. Pam said you're lying. Bet you're knocked up aren't you. I told her no, I wasn't, it was just my monthlies.

Then she opened the drawer and said well what's this then and pulled the test packet out. And I told her to fuck off. She lifted it above her head and said I'm gonna tell Mam. So I grabbed her and then we started on each other in the bedroom. I could have killed her. Don't tell her please I cried. She needs to know Pam said. I squeezed on her wrist and it made her hand go blue. Told her she was a grass. And you're nowt but a slag she said. And we rolled onto the bed clawing at each other. The door went and Mam was stood there. We stopped scrapping and went quiet. What's all this about. All that noise. You two carrying on. Nowt we said. Just messing about. You're lying you two and I can see it. What's that behind your back our Pam. Are you smoking again. No, Pam said. Not hiding anything. Mam pushed me to one side and pulled the test out of her hands. She's pregnant Pam said and looked at me. I wanted to twat her. Mam shook her head. You, you're going nowhere tonight she said to Pam. And you, get yourself downstairs we need to sort this out. She put her hand on my shoulder and I started to cry.

*

Alma arranged to speak to the Headmaster at Buttershaw Upper School after he was informed about Andrea's pregnancy. She wore her Sunday best and paid for a shampoo and set that morning. It was important that he didn't think that they were *that* kind of family. As she walked out of the house John Brian shouted after her.

Where the fucking hell are you going looking like that? he said. Don't I get an invite?

Mind your own, she replied and slammed the gate behind her.

The school was a vast building with white panels and large windows at the front. It had a swimming pool, its own theatre, and playing fields. The roof was flat and classrooms had modern fittings. The foyer had a polished floor and the sound from Alma's shoes ricocheted as she walked towards the Headmaster's office. She sat on a wooden chair and stared at the posters outside the School Nurse's room. One had a photograph of a pregnant man staring at the camera, it said WOULD YOU BE MORE CAREFUL IF IT WAS YOU THAT GOT PREGNANT? Alma raised her eyebrows and chuckled.

Wouldn't they just, she said.

A voice echoed down the hall.

Mrs Dunbar, he said. Ready to see you now.

The Headmaster beckoned her in to his room and sat behind the desk. He pushed his glasses up the bridge of his nose.

This really is quite serious, he said. Your daughter is underage.

I know that, Alma tutted. But there's not much we can do about it now. I've promised to help her as much as I can.

Do you have any idea who the father is?

No. She won't tell me. Or anyone for that matter. Keeps herself to herself.

Andrea isn't a bad student, he said. Her teachers tell me she has quite a talent for English. However, she can be difficult at times. I hope that this spell at Barkerend will improve her attitude.

He straightened his tie and began to fill in a form.

Don't think she likes school that much, Alma said. Takes after me. I started work at fourteen.

Well, yes. I understand that. But there is a requirement for all minors – and she is still a minor – to complete their CSE examinations. Perhaps she may be better suited to a trade?

I should hope so.

Alma sat with her handbag on her knee and folded her gloves over the handle.

What's this new school like, then?

It's called Barkerend School for Unmarried Mothers, he continued. A place where she will be tutored through the next stage of her education until her baby is born. She will get all of the support she needs, and importantly, it will protect her from any of the cruel names or intimidation that she might experience from her classmates here.

Our Andrea can look after herself, make no mistake.

I'm sure she can. But after the child is born I want her to know that she is welcome to come back here to finish her education. It's just, well, much easier if she leaves for the time being.

Will she get a bus pass to take her there?

Yes, the council will send you one. And a social worker will be in touch with you shortly.

Oh, will they, now? Alma rolled her eyes. That's the last thing we need.

It's just part of the process, nothing to worry about Mrs Dunbar, he said. Now, I just need you to sign this form to say she will stay in a mother-and-baby home permanently for a month before the baby is due.

He held out the form in front of Alma.

I'm not signing that. She's staying with me. Andrea's my daughter. And I'll look after her.

The Headmaster paused.

We aren't trying to take her away from you Mrs Dunbar, it's more for her own safety. Some of the girls at Barkerend, well, they have been disowned by their families. The shame of being unwed is too much so they are sent away until an adoption can be arranged.

But the bairn's due before spring, Alma said. I'm not having her in there on her own. It's just not right.

That night Alma sat Andrea down with John Brian after they had finished eating. Andrea was subdued all night in anticipation of the argument that was about to erupt.

John Brian had spent the day in the Cap and Bells and was well oiled. He scarfed his mashed potato, belched and made a gurgling noise when he drank his brew.

I've summat to tell you, Alma said. Well, our Andrea has summat to tell you.

She don't tell me owt, he said. What do I know?

Andrea tried to say the words but her mouth was dry and she couldn't speak.

27

Sorry . . . can't say it . . . she said and looked at Alma. Mam, tell him.

Tell me what?

She's pregnant, Alma said.

What?! You're fucking up the duff?

John Brian threw his cutlery across the table and kicked his chair over.

Are you bloody joking? he yelled. You're only a child.

Andrea backed towards the corner of the room. Tears started rolling down her cheeks.

Didn't mean for it to happen, she said.

We've had all these letters about you skiving off school, he said. And you've been carrying on with some dirty sod and got knocked up.

It's not like that. Caught on by accident.

Accident?! How is *shagging* an accident?! You stupid little cow. I'll wrap my belt round your fucking legs.

She hid behind Alma, who had pushed her body between Andrea's and his.

Who is it? I'll kill him.

None of your bloody business, Alma shouted. Now go to bed. We can talk about it in the morning.

She folded her arms and wedged herself in front of him.

I have a right to know, he said.

John Brian's leg dipped to one side as he released a noxious fart and staggered towards the front door.

He doesn't live round here, Andrea replied.

You're lying. I can see it in your face. You can't fucking lie to save your life. Now, I'm off back to the pub … rather play darts than listen to you lot.

*

Each day Andrea caught the bus to Barkerend School from Reevy Road. She kept Craig's ring on a chain around her neck and wore it over the top of her pullover. Sometimes she wore it on her ring finger. They had barely spoken since that day in the market, and on the odd occasion where they passed in the street, he walked over to the other side of the road and turned away from her.

The days were long and sleepy, and even though the sickness had abated, she felt tired most of the time, and often ravenous. During the first few months she felt queasy every day although packets of Seabrook's calmed the rocking waves and she quickly gained weight. At only five feet two inches she was a small girl, and wore large hand-me-down jumpers and stretch pants to conceal the bump as the leaves began to fall.

Although she had finished at Buttershaw Upper School word quickly spread about her baby. Gangs of lads sniggered at her as she walked to the bus stop. One of them, Sean, followed her past the shops every day, walking a few feet behind her to wind her up. He lived on Barden Avenue, just a few minutes' walk from the Arbor.

Eh, Andrea. Why are you ignoring me? he shouted as she wandered past him one afternoon.

I'm not. Just minding my own. Like you should.

He stood up from the wall and started following her down the street.

That's a big belly you've got, he said.

Really? she replied. I hadn't noticed.

Oh, she's got a sense of humour!

He turned his face to the lads and started laughing.

Leave me alone.

Who's the Daddy then?

Nowt to do wi you, she said. Your B.O. fucking stinks.

Sean pushed his shoulders back and pulled up the collar on his shirt. Heard it might be one of your neighbours.

Look, if you don't fuck off I'll tell David.

David. *As if.*

Sean shook his head. He pushed Andrea against the bush and stroked her face.

You're not bad looking you know, he said. I mean it. You've got lovely eyes.

Andrea's heart started beating faster. The rage began to rise from her gut.

Sean ... you doilum. Get off me before I batter you.

He pushed her further into the bush and pulled at the necklace, it broke and the ring rolled onto the ground. He grabbed it as she reached down to catch it.

What's this? A ring? Engaged are we? Now who's the lucky man?

Andrea started shouting at him and lunged at his face with her fist. He quickly jumped out of the way.

Not much of a fighter! Are you a southpaw?

It wasn't the first time Sean had done this. He was only flirting with her and even though they often argued in the street, he always backed down.

Just get lost. Gimme it back.

She tried to grab the ring from his fist, Sean swatted her away. He held it in front of her face.

You'll get your head kicked in, she said.

Allus thought one day you'd be mine, he grinned. That it would be *my* ring on your finger. How's my heart ever going to repair now?

Just fuck off you menc. I mean it, she shouted.

As they wrestled with each other a car pulled up behind them. Sean's mate, Dowkey, wound down the window and shouted for them to get in.

Wanna lift? he said. Where are you off to?

The bus stop, she replied. And I'll miss it unless he gives me my ring back, the thieving twat.

Come on then, get in. I'll give you a ride.

Andrea jumped into the back of the car and Sean squashed in next to her. He pinched her arm and dropped the ring into her top pocket as they sped towards the main road. Dowkey put his foot down on the accelerator and black smoke belched from the exhaust pipe. They tore past the Crescent, dodging children that scattered across the road. As they took a sharp right a blue light flashed in the rear view mirror. Dowkey slammed his foot down further and told them to run as soon as he braked. At that point Andrea saw the hot wires hanging from underneath the steering wheel and realised that Dowkey's car wasn't his car after all.

The police sirens kicked in and as Dowkey span the wheel Andrea and Sean shook in the backseat as the car rolled over onto its side, and wrapped around a lamp post. Andrea's body went limp for a split second, and her side ached from the weight of Sean's body that crushed her as she lay concealed beneath him. She was pulled out of the steaming car by policemen who lifted her onto a grass verge by the van. A group of people congregated around the crushed car. Sean's head was bleeding. Dowkey was nowhere to be seen. She felt a dull pain in the base of her stomach; she knew that something wasn't right.

*

They told her it was small enough to fit in the palm of her hand. When she came round from the anaesthetic she made out the shape of Alma's body sitting at the foot of the bed. The doctors had given her pain killers and a drip was connected to her hand.

Andrea stared at the bunch of carnations next to her pillow, reached for the sick carton, and wept between the retching.

Don't want to see it. It'll only make things worse ... just wanna go home.

Alma sat next to her and held her hand.

Here, she said. Have some water. It'll all come out in the wash.

She tilted the cup towards her cracked lips and dripped the fluid into her mouth.

I really ... don't know ...

Sweat poured from Andrea's brow and Alma covered her feet with a blanket.

Me head's spinning, she said.

Alma looked after her in the following weeks, and the long days sitting at home in front of the television only amplified the horror. Her mind locked onto the crash, her baby, the hospital, and the medical staff who said it was for the best. Fast forward, rewind. Play. Pause. Play again. The trauma of a tape that didn't stop.

Maybe school will help, Alma suggested, as she brought her tea in bed. They said they'll have you back. You can start again. Fresh over.

I don't wanna go back.

You can't stay here for the rest of your life, Alma said. Everyone has to finish school. You don't want to end up like half the people round here. Not being able to get a job or read and write properly.

She knew that Alma was right. After a few sulks and strops she reluctantly agreed to return to Buttershaw Upper School in October 1975. Unlike her previous years, where she tried to dodge class every day, this time she turned up early each morning, with completed homework in her bag.

Her teachers were confident they could provide a positive influence on the pupils; the majority lived on the estate. She studied the curriculum – French, Science, Maths, History, Geography, English, and Domestic Science. Her Geography teacher remarked that *Andrea must realise that the world exists outside of Yorkshire: D–*. In Religious Instruction, her teacher was less than impressed, *Andrea is not God. She must come to terms with this: D*. The previous year her Domestic Science tutor had no recorded register of her presence throughout the whole term. But when she returned, aged fifteen, the lessons provided a focus away from the chaos at home and even though she didn't understand most of it, she enjoyed Biology and spent sleepy afternoons staring at the jars of pickled brains, rabbits' feet and dead butterflies that lined the walls in the lab. Her aptitude for English and Drama became apparent when she started achieving some of the highest grades in the school. It was a mystery to her parents. And an even bigger mystery to her.

*

They used to say I had a chip on my shoulder. Whatever that means. I couldn't ever work that out but I know I always felt that I wasn't as good as other people. I was angry. Some teachers used to get cross and say that I'd never amount to anything. The lads in class said I should just get married and have kids and be a housewife. They told me I was thick when I couldn't add up. Used to get stuck in class, wanted to run out and go home. It was hot in the classrooms and I felt sick but they wouldn't let me leave. So I stopped going in the end.

They couldn't tell me anything new anyway.

I already knew it.

Careers Advice said I could be a shop assistant, mill worker, nanny or hairdresser. All of those sounded shit. I asked them can I be a writer and they laughed at me. What someone from here, a writer. You're living in cloud-cuckoo-land they said. Only the brightest get to do jobs like that. And there's no jobs for writers in Bradford. Don't get your hopes up lass. But I like writing I said. It's the only thing I'm good at. If you study hard you might become a primary school teacher or work in the bank. But that means no messing about they said. You have to be realistic.

At least I knew where I stood.

*

Andrea spent each lunch break in Colin Smith's classroom. He was the Art teacher who played classical music to the bullied pupils as they ate their packed lunches. Colin talked to them about music and art, his room was covered in posters: Andy Warhol's *Campbell's Soup Cans*, Pablo Picasso's *Guernica* and *Madame Butterfly* at the Royal Albert Hall. Shelves were decorated with ceramics and spider plants, books were piled up in the corners, coated in paint splats and glue. It was a place for the quiet ones to hide.

Colin told some of his colleagues about a girl called Andrea Dunbar. He had seen a copy of an essay she had written as a punishment for not bringing in the correct ingredients in Domestic Science class. She spent her detention period in his classroom and he supervised her as she wrote the words *Why I Don't Like Cookery* across the top of the page. Her teacher Mrs Brown informed her that it had to be written neatly on two pages during her lunch break.

Andrea did as she was asked and completed the task in half an hour. What she wrote – how cooking buns was a middle-class hobby, and how joints of meat were far more practical for big families on Buttershaw – was communicated in a witty polemic that compared the impracticalities of her home life to the useless pursuit of cooking a raspberry pavlova.

When the essay was passed around the staffroom the day after to howls of laughter the Head of Drama, Tony Priestley, was astonished at what he saw in front of him. She was the shy girl that Colin had told him about and he hadn't noticed her before, but it was obvious to him that she had a special gift for saying the right thing. And she was funny, too. He tracked her down after registration one day and asked if she'd like to join his class. What happened over the coming months would change Andrea's life forever.

During English and Drama lessons, which often focused on Shakespeare, and were confusing to Andrea at the best of times, Tony suggested that she wrote about her home-life instead.

I want you to think about what you see and hear at home, he said. Write something set in your kitchen. Try and write it in the way you talk.

Thought we were supposed to be writing *Macbeth* set in Bradford, she replied. Can't get me head around that at all. Can't understand what he's on about half the time.

Andrea pushed her copy of *Macbeth* to one side and stared at the empty page in front of her.

Can't work out the language, or why everyone laughs at the parts that are meant to be serious.

Tony pulled a chair up and spoke to her in a hushed voice.

This was written years ago, so it's not surprising that it's hard to comprehend, he said. I don't want you to worry about it. Forget Shakespeare for the time being. He can wait. Write about Buttershaw. Write about what you know.

Don't know where to start.

How about you write about what happened at Barkerend School? How did they treat you there? What were the other girls like?

Most of em were idiots, Andrea said.

Write about you. Your life is interesting, even if you think it isn't. You look surprised but you have to realise that all plays start somewhere. Start keeping notes on what you hear. Write about where you live and who your parents are. Your brothers and sisters. The things you feel.

What, like a diary?

Yes. Just like that. Try and write every day. Even if it's just ten minutes before bed. Do that for a week and we'll see if there's something we can pull out of it.

Andrea frowned.

I already have pads full of writing, she said. Just never showed it to anyone before.

See, I knew you were a writer already, he replied.

Throughout the lessons she read *Pygmalion* and learned how to format her writing by taping the words she had written and transcribing the lines as they were played back. *Maria Marten*, or *Murder in the Red Barn*, was a particular favourite of hers. She stood up in class one day to tell them about why she liked it.

This play was based on a murder in 1827. It's called a melodrama.

Tony raised his hand.

And what does melodrama mean?

Erm.

Andrea paused and turned red.

Come on, you know this. You told me last week. It's a . . .

Oh yeah. It's a play where lots of things happen and the characters get angry with each other.

Yes, you're right, Tony said. They exaggerate how they feel through their actions and speech. Continue.

Andrea cleared her throat and began to read from the words she had written the previous night.

Maria Marten is about a man called William who seduces then murders a girl called Maria in a red barn and buries her body beneath the floor. It happened in real life and William Corder was hanged for killing her, she continued. The council skinned his body and made a real book all about the court case with his skin on the cover.

The class started laughing.

No wonder you like it, one of them shouted.

I'm surprised that you picked this title out of all the books in the library. Why did you choose it? Tony said.

Because I like horror. When I read the back of it and heard about the book made out of skin then I thought the play might be good. And when I read it, it was.

That's interesting to hear, Tony said. I'll bring you something to read next week that you might like. It's called *Carrie* by Stephen King. You can borrow it as long as you bring it back.

Over the following weeks Andrea re-read *Carrie* a hundred times, staying up late every night to finish it again. She borrowed every Stephen King book from the library and read them cover to cover.

With encouragement from Tony and Colin she began to develop the early drafts for her play based on an autobiographical argument scene about a girl who denies she's pregnant after her sister betrays her. A flaming row erupts when her father threatens to beat her and her mother steps in to defend her.

Tony was so impressed by the quality of her dialogue and characters that he urged her to carry on. Instead of reading Shakespeare in each lesson Andrea worked on her play. Tony suggested that she wrote another scene. This time she created a car chase and what happens after the girl accepts a lift one night and finds out that the vehicle is stolen. In the script the police give chase, the car crashes, the girl is arrested and loses her baby.

A full version was presented on tape for her CSE, along with a script of twenty pages. It received an A grade from the examination board.

She called it *The Arbor*.

2

Paper Sheets

It's been so cold this winter. My toes are like ice cubes. Two pairs of tights and a thermal vest, can't keep my hands warm.

It was −17 in Yorkshire the other day. Dad says the canal froze in Shipley. Nobody's got any money and there's nothing to graft because everything's been pawned.

There's strikes everywhere and the shop shelves are empty. Even the farm animals are eating each other because they've got no food either.

Eileen's mate had horse stew for tea. She said it tasted alright, a bit like beef. Horse is half the price so some up here have to eat it otherwise they'd starve.

Mrs Henshaw had a baby last week at the Infirmary and there was hardly anyone there. She delivered it herself on paper sheets because the hospital had run out of money.

Even the bus drivers are picketing. So if we want to go into town we have to walk, in this weather. People in London can't get their bins emptied, so it must be bad.

Yorkshire TV is on strike, so we've had no channel three for two months. The worst thing about it all is not that I'm hungry, cold or skint. I'm more upset about missing Crossroads *to be honest. It's just not on.*

*

Andrea left Buttershaw Upper School with three CSE passes and started work at Bowling Mill on Manchester Road. The vast building stretched across south Bradford's skyline. It was one of the largest in the city and often operated day and night. The noise and smoke that belched from its chimneys caused a pea-soup smog that hung over the railway tracks.

One of Alma's relatives worked regular shifts in the mill and spoke with the overseers, who offered Andrea a trial shift. She took to the job with ease, her work speed was impressive, and she quickly gained the attention of the older women on the floor who gave her a lesson on working the French Comb. Her fingers were fast and nimble and within a month or two she was placed permanently onto combing, earning £47 a week, a solid wage for the time. It took gruelling shifts to bring a decent pay packet home, but she put in the extra hours like the other young women in the mill.

Some of the workers feared their jobs were precarious, and

often talked on their lunch breaks about worsted mills closing across the Ridings. Ten had folded in the previous month. Suppliers could buy wool cheaper in India. Alarm bells were ringing; there was something foul in the air.

Andrea's father, John Brian, had been a wool warehouse-man, and his wife, Alma, a worsted twister. Her grandfathers were also wool combers. She followed generations of Dunbars straight onto the shop floor. Alongside wool sorters, combers were some of the most skilled workers in the trade.

Each day Andrea took the prepared wool, combed and straightened it through fine pins, and removed short fibres and vegetable matter from the fleece. The wool was drawn off from the machine in a long continuous sliver and she coiled the noil into a pile. The combing pins were heated to soften grease in the wool, helping the fibre slide through more easily.

Andrea looked after a group of machines which constantly lapped, snagged and chewed up the wool onto the York Stone floor which bled oil and grease in summer months. That winter it was so cold she sprayed anti-freeze on the windows before she started work. Her fingers seized up in the hoar frost's bite.

The boiler houses that overlooked the combing floor were filthy, chambers of intense heat fired by coke and coal. Dirty men with soot-black faces and dripping with sweat shovelled fuel into the furnace throughout the day. Their flat caps and clothes were covered in grime, the whites of their eyes and

43

teeth the only glimmer of light in the place. The muck permeated all corners of the buildings. Rats made cosy nests in the skirting and lived off workers' food droppings.

Each morning immigrant workers pushed crates of wool washed in the boiler house into the lifts on crates. They were wheeled across the floor and fastened up next to Andrea's comb. Some told her the raw wool was crawling with fleas and ticks when it arrived; they treated the fleece to remove the dirt. They had been given anthrax vaccinations and advised that she should have one too. The skins were grotesque and often riddled with scabies. Goats' legs were found rotting in the shipments. Feet and tails. Mites and muck. Filth ran out of every pore. It took hours to get clean after a shift. Her hands and clothes were covered in machine oil; she chain-smoked to block out the stench and swore she would wear white for the rest of her life when she stopped working at the mill.

The shop floor's noise was overwhelming for new staff. Many workers were deaf from the lack of hearing protection, or had permanent ringing in their ears from the clatter of the looms. Women sang to each other over the rattle and hum; it was easier to hear notes over the constant din of the machinery. Lip-reading was commonplace. They revelled in close, personal and intimate conversations.

Marriage, children, relationships, sex.

The latest gossip.

Who owed money to who.

Andrea wore headphones but the heat from wearing them

after a morning shift made sweat drip over her eyebrows and caused her hair to frizz. She picked up lip-reading and made friends with old-timers who had worked there since school. They were hardened women, the toughest in Bradford who had lived through unrelenting times. Some had missing fingers eaten by comb mouths. Others had scoliosis from hefting barrels since their youth. Many had children and husbands to feed, and managed to work double-shifts twice a week.

Andrea worked on her feet every day, lurching over the comb, feeding wool into buzzing jaws on the metal plate. She watched rollers eat the wool and fed it onto a leather apron before spooling it into a large barrel can. Thousands of yards rolled into cans. She stood in the same spot six days a week, with the clunk of machinery and clanking metal echoing around her.

Doing what her parents had done.

Doing what her grandparents had done.

Lifting, weaving, and combing as day turned into night.

*

The rumours from the canteen turned out to be true. Wage packets were docked by £8 leaving barely enough to put food on the table or pay the rent. The workers complained that their children were hungry after jam and bread for tea every night, their growing feet blistered from too-small shoes. In the early seventies they had worked twelve-hour shifts and six-day weeks. Now they didn't know how many hours they'd get from one week to the next. More than three thousand textile workers had been laid off in Bradford alone.

Andrea sat with Joan, one of the women who worked on the floor, as they emptied their pay packets onto the table after clocking off.

That's half what I got last week, she said. Don't know how I'll manage.

Schools are shutting early, so I have to get the kids looked after.

Joan crossed her legs and rubbed at her dry hands, still white from the disinfectant she had scrubbed the floors with.

And as for the shopping, well, I couldn't even buy toilet paper yesterday. Using newspaper to wipe my backside. I'm sick of it.

They're all on strike, Andrea said. Maybe we should go on one an all.

Fat lotta good that'd do. Him upstairs would be happy to see the back of us.

Did you hear gravediggers have stopped, you know, burying people?

Andrea pointed to the front page of a newspaper on the serving hatch.

They reckon all the bodies are in a warehouse somewhere. That they'll bury em at sea. There's hell on.

Well, summat's got to give. Can't go on like this.

Joan pulled out a list from her pocket, with a line of rotas for the following week.

I've a spare shift for you on Thursday night, it's a late one. Six while two. They're running a half week so we're doing nights until it picks up again. You'll need to catch a taxi home.

I'll take owt I can get, Andrea replied.

Have you thought about what might happen, if they shut this place down?

Suppose I'll sign on. But I'd rather work. Dunno what else I'd do . . . could try looking for factory jobs. Or cleaning.

You know what, this is the only job I've ever done. Me whole life in here.

Joan opened up her bag, pulled out a mirror and rubbed a speck of grease from her cheek.

I'm telling you, she said. It's all going to shit.

Allus thought I'd be a writer . . .

Andrea's eyes sparkled as the afternoon light caught the kitchen's reflection.

Teachers at school said I were good. Tony and Colin sent my play off to YTV. Nowt came of it though. The woman there said I needed to try harder.

Really? Never knew that, Joan said. What sort of things do you write?

Just write down what I see and hear. Normal people's lives. Haven't written owt since I started here. All piled up under me bed.

Joan reached into her bag and pulled out a battered copy of *No Darkness for Love*.

Always thought I had a book in me, she said. Barbara Cartland. Now that's what I call a writer.

*

Andrea worked into the early hours of the morning and caught a taxi home. She ordered it from the office foyer and a firm on Leeds Road, Solar Cars, sent a driver. The same one arrived each night.

For the first few weeks Andrea sat in the backseat of the taxi, and stared out of the window as the signposts for Canterbury, Shelf and Wibsey flashed by. She didn't notice him at first. He didn't talk much, but one morning she caught his eyes through the wing mirror, they were blacker than anthracite, with long dark eyelashes that reached to his eyebrows. Sometimes he talked to her and turned down his radio, which played Indian music from the speakers. A pendant with a gold fringe was fastened above the mirror. Her cheeks turned red when he spoke to her.

He told her his name was Yousaf.

Sometimes they talked all the way back to Buttershaw. Early one morning, after she had finished her shift, he opened the front door of his car and told her to get in.

You still looking for work? he asked.

Yeah. Don't know what's going on down here. It's been dreadful over the past few weeks.

She smiled at him and batted the orange air freshener that swung from the car's roof.

He turned the radio down and cleared his throat.

Well, I was thinking, we need someone, a good person. For the office. They have to know Bradford, all the areas.

Not sure if I'm right for that. Can't even drive.

His car rattled up through Little Horton as he headed towards the traffic lights.

You'd be good, he said. I know this. I can teach you the area. All in the A–Z. You just need to be quick at answering. We need pretty ladies in the office. Ali's no good with the accents.

Yousaf laughed and put the car into second gear.

The office is up Leeds Road. That's miles away.

I'll pick you up. Take you home. Not bad money. Cash in hand. And, you can work whatever shifts, but you have to do some nights. You're tempted, no?

I'll have a think about it, she said. Bet you're just offering so you can see more of me.

Andrea crossed her legs and Yousaf stared at her.

You know, I worked in the mills when I first came here. But I make more money on the taxi than I ever did sorting wool. My family, they're from a village called Waisa. Small place. About an hour from Islamabad. My father, he works in the rice fields. But there's not much work there.

Is that why you came to Bradford then? she asked.

Well, yeah. They called us *gastarbeiters*. Pakistan is in the Commonwealth. They needed workers for the mills over here . . .

He indicated left on the roundabout and slowed down as he approached Buttershaw.

49

Me and my brothers, they gave us citizenship, he continued. We ended up here, working the filthy jobs with wool.

She rubbed her eyes and yawned as the waves of tiredness washed over her.

Feel sorry for people who do that. It's grim.

The British don't want to do it. So we do it instead. Very hard when we first came here. You know, I'd never been to a city before I came to Bradford, he laughed. It was a shock, I tell you.

He paused and pointed under his seat.

Underneath here, I've got a baseball bat. Kept getting robbed when I first started, not easy dealing with the drunks, he said. But you, you're my best customer. Nice eyes.

Andrea started work at Solar Cars the following week, and learned how to collect calls, shout at the drunks and get their money up front. By the time her first few shifts were completed she knew each postcode inside out, and kept the drivers in line across the fleet. Just before dawn was the hardest time, cigarettes and tea couldn't keep her awake. But the boss gave her bonuses and Yousaf brought her piping hot samosas, filled with cumin and potato.

It wasn't such a bad place to work after all. As her shifts at Solar Cars increased, she noticed Yousaf staring at her from inside his cab, over the road. Long glances across the street.

*

None of the men on Buttershaw look like him. He's so handsome I can't even make eye contact.

When I finished work at the mill, covered in grease, he looked at me as if I was wearing diamonds and a mink fur coat.

No man has ever made me feel like this.

I can't say no to him.

When Dad found out he said he would kill me and him. There are only white people in Buttershaw he said and white people are supposed to go out with other white people, but especially not Pakistanis.

When he drives me home sometimes we walk around together in the early hours of the day. Everyone is asleep then. He waits around the corner until I've walked in the front door.

The other night we got stopped by police on the street, they asked where we were going and followed us in the car. What's it to you I said. Yousaf said Let me speak to them, don't you get involved. Why are they stopping us? It's none of their bloody business.

Keep quiet he said. I'll talk. So the policeman took out his pad and said Can I ask what you're both doing at this time of night. Just having a nice walk, Yousaf laughed. We work together. Oh I bet you do the policeman said We know all about your type.

What've I done wrong? I'm only walking down the street.

Can I check your licence and insurance?

Yes Yousaf said I have it here in my glove compartment, I'm a taxi driver. Oh, said the policeman Well why isn't your taxi licence plate displayed at the back. Because I'm off duty he said. Like I said just having a walk.

We've had reports of burglaries around here the policeman said. You can't be too careful . . .

I wanted to shout but knew I had to shut my mouth. Then I said it.

Well if YOU did your job properly stopping robbers instead of stopping people like us then it wouldn't happen, would it.

Yousaf turned to him. Ignore her, she's had too much to drink he said. That's why I'm bringing her home. The policeman frowned at me and got into his car. You're gonna get me locked up one of these days Yousaf said.

The other week Sharon and Pauline started giving us grief when they saw us go in the shop together and shouted over the road. Does he make you walk behind him, they said. Are you gonna marry him then? You can cook, clean, and have his kids for the rest of your life. He won't let you out.

Then Pauline said You'll be wearing a sari next and started singing Bud bud ding ding tickets please. I nearly smashed her bastard face in. It's not like that I said. And yes, I am bothering with him. Eugh bet he smells of curry you don't know where he's been they said. And Yousaf just looked ahead and kept walking.

The lads call him Useless Yousaf. When a Pakistani family moved on our street they had their windows put in every night. That's why there aren't any on Buttershaw. Yousaf's is the only brown face on the estate. We have to be careful up here.

*

It was a bright clear day on the Arbor and Andrea was sorting through boxes in her bedroom, clearing out old clothes and hand-me-downs. Pam had given her a silver dress that didn't suit her and she pulled it on over her bra and thick tights.

Right chuffed with this, Andrea said. I'll wear it down the Mecca.

She danced in front of the window and started singing along to *Night Fever* on the wireless that blasted through the walls from David's room.

Look at this, my old school books. Think I'll keep em.

Yousaf leafed through her jotters and lay back on the bed. You have good schools in Bradford, he said. I only ever went to school once. Teachers gave me a note for my parents saying I needed books before I could go back.

You had to buy your own books?

Andrea pulled the dress over her head.

They couldn't afford it, too much money. My country is poor. They kept me at home instead, to work on the farm.

Can you read and write?

Not really. Can read road signs, do receipts. But not much more than that. Watch lots of films, listen to radio. That's why I worked in the mill, could only do textiles or driving because I can't read well. People . . . they laugh at me when I tell them. The English don't know what poverty is, he said. There's no dole office in Pakistan. We have to pay for the doctor, drugs. No sanitation. You don't know how lucky you are over here.

Outside on the main shopping parade a bell tower rang on the hour, its ominous toll echoed through the streets and down into the valley. It was clear to hear when the wind blew in from the west.

Yousaf and Andrea walked downstairs and sat down on the sofa next to John Brian, who was watching TV. He'd been bickering with David again. His youngest son, Stephen, had died years ago and David had argued non-stop with his father in the weeks following his death. Every row returned to the same one that began back then. It was never-ending.

Father and son scowled at each other from across the living room and Yousaf attempted to make small talk with them.

Nice day today, he said. How've you been?

They ignored him.

Yousaf watched the television as John Brian and David started to shout at each other.

You don't even care, David said. Your own son, run over.

He was flat down on the road, waiting for a lorry to hit him. John Brian said. What did he expect? Shouldn't have bloody done it in the first place, should he. I mean, what kind of game is that?!!

Listen to yourself, going on, David said. You're nowt but a bastard.

Takes one to know one, John Brian replied.

And a drunk. Fuck off to bed, Dad. It's the only place left for you.

The room fell silent.

Maybe you could sort this out, you know. Talk it over. Make friends? Yousaf offered. It's not worth fighting over.

Andrea rattled about in the kitchen and laughed with Kathy as they dried wet pots. The quiet moment was broken when David turned to Yousaf and screamed at the top of his voice.

Who the fucking hell do you think you are, coming up here and telling me what to do? I'll bash your fucking Paki head in.

It's not my fault I'm a Paki, Yousaf said.

Yes it fucking *is*! David replied.

Andrea slammed the back door and came storming into the room.

What the hell are you shouting at him for?

I'm not fucking shouting. He started it!

David pointed at Yousaf who shrugged his shoulders and lifted up his hands.

Only trying to help, Yousaf replied.

Well *don't*, she said. Let em bang their own heads together. They deserve each other.

Andrea pushed Yousaf into the doorway and grabbed her jacket.

Get your stuff. We're off. I've had enough, she said. Can't live here. It's driving me mad.

Yousaf paused as she continued walking towards his car, through the grass on the Arbor.

You can live with me. If you want, he said. Just for a bit. But, you know, my house has no furniture.

Anything has to be better than this, she replied.

There's nowhere to sleep, the mattress is on the floor. Hardly any curtains. I've only beer crates for chairs. No carpet. Shaffi lives in the top room. He snores all night.

Andrea sniggered.

Oh, I've already heard him through the floorboards.

The cooker. It doesn't really work. And the water pipes rattle.

Are you trying to say you don't want me to come?

No. Not that. It's just, people might talk. My sister, she wouldn't approve. I'll need to hide you. And the baby.

He paused and held her hand.

They sat in the front of the car and he reached over towards her belly. He stroked the small bump under her shirt and rested his head in her lap.

He smiled and whispered to her.

Still our secret?

Our secret, she replied.

3

The Next One Could Be Innocent

It was three months before her baby was due. Andrea finished working at Solar Cars and hardly slept in the months leading up to the birth. The baby pressed on her bladder with its feet, and she could feel it kicking and moving in the early hours. She lay on the bed, staring up at the patterns that ran across the ceiling from the traffic outside and waited for Yousaf to return. It would take some negotiation to go shopping that day.

Andrea had arranged to meet Eileen in town. They often wrote to each other. Eileen's son was a year old and a handful at the best of times. She brought him with her that day. A list for the baby had been pinned above the kitchen sink for a month; steriliser, nappies, swaddling and booties. Alma and John Brian bought her a pram; a second-hand Silver Cross from a friend of a friend. It was cream with a hood and had bright shining wheels. It sat in the hall by the draughty front door.

They met on Ivegate. It was months since they had seen each other. Eileen wore high waisted trousers, a black velour top and a short leather jacket with lapels. Her hair was cut into a feather fringe, longer at the back, with highlights on top.

Andrea scoffed when she saw her and hid her laughs behind her hand.

So you're a punk now, are you?

Just updating my look. Have to keep the fellas interested.

Eileen sashayed her hips and flicked her head to one side.

How've you been?

Not bad.

Andrea stared at the ground.

Shall we go to market then?

Eileen tucked the blanket into her son's pushchair and they began to walk up the steep hill. A line of Black Maria police vans parked on the street with advertising posters fixed to the doors. One said THE NEXT ONE COULD BE INNOCENT. Another contained an image of handwriting, with the words HELP US STOP THE RIPPER KILLING AGAIN in bold with a phone number underneath.

They were all at it in Littlewood's last week, Eileen laughed. Posters everywhere and speakers playing that Geordie voice. They reckon he's from up there. There were a stall, giving stuff out – look, I bought an alarm thing and this . . .

She pulled out a Rapel Stink Pen from her bag.

What the hell's that? Andrea said.

You keep it in your jacket or trouser pocket. Then, when he creeps up on you, you press it. And it fucking stinks. Lets off an egg-bomb.

Nice to see someone's cashing in. The whole thing gives me the jitters. Them poor lasses. The one last week were awful. On her way to work at the factory.

Andrea stood in front of the van and read the words out loud. *Who is he? Flush him out for us. He doesn't deserve your pity.*

What happened to her? Eileen asked.

They found her on a football pitch, under the clock tower in Halifax. He'd been at her with an hammer. They found her body crouched over on all fours.

Andrea rubbed on her back and pointed to a bench.

Need to sit down, me back's aching to buggery, she said.

What a way to go . . .

Eileen tapped her feet on the floor and stared at a man across the way dressed in a brown monk's habit and sandals.

She had bite marks. Reckon he's got a gap in his teeth. Stabbed her twenty-one times.

Dunno about you but I'm scared, Eileen said. He keeps doing it round here. That's only three miles from Buttershaw.

Maybe it's someone we know? Andrea said.

What, like your old man?

How could that appen, he's got no teeth.

They both sniggered and wandered into the market hall,

past butcher's row where trays of chops were being prepared for the weekend's meat raffle. Kidney and liver, black pudding for breakfast. Tripe and faggots, brawn and kippers. Beaks and feet. Arseholes and lungs. Buckets of blood. Buckets of tongues. Food for real men.

Legs of mutton swung behind the counter, and behind them Eileen glimpsed a Page Three poster hidden from the customers. Dolly birds with big jugs. Short skirts and painted-on eyelashes. Sandy tits on a sunny beach. The kind of girls that didn't talk back.

They're bloody shameless, Eileen said. Our Roy's got a full wall of Linda Lusardi in his bedroom.

They walked towards the baby stalls, through the crowds that jostled for knock-down fruit.

How's things with Yousaf then?

Oh. Alright. You know. The usual.

Andrea walked faster as Eileen struggled to keep pace.

Is he ready to be a Dad?

Dunno about that. He's very . . . protective. Doesn't like me going out on my own.

It can bring a funny side out, Eileen added. Have you made any friends up there?

They're all *his* friends. His mate lives in the house. He keeps an eye on me when Yousaf's driving. But, he's alright. Makes me laugh . . . not sure about the frills on this, she said.

Andrea picked up a bonnet from the counter and began to finger the lace and ribbons.

Allus thought you two got on.

We did. It were fine before. But, you know. Living with him is different to going out with him, she handed a note to the till and waited for her change. We've been rowing a lot.

You row with everyone.

I know. But it's not like I'm looking for it.

What do you mean by that?

Just, it blows up out of nowhere. A few nights back I were washing up and he came in, he were in a mood as it'd been quiet at work ... I don't know what I did wrong, but before I knew it he were throwing his weight around, telling me I'd caused him all this bother ...

You don't have to stay.

Eileen put her arm around her.

If it gets bad, just walk out ...

I *want* it to work. Have my own life. But his temper scares me sometimes. Gets out of hand.

Andrea walked up the steps towards the fabric stall and picked up a pile of baby blankets, opened them up and squeezed the wool.

I'm here, you know that.

Even coming out today I had to lie. Pretended I had an appointment. He doesn't like me having friends ...

Why didn't you tell me before? I could've helped you.

Don't like talking about it, Andrea replied. Wish it'd go away on its own. Anyhow, I've decided to go back to the mill.

Thought you said you'd never go back.

I can earn good money, even just the odd shift here and there. Joan offered me a few hours. He's not happy about that of course.

It'll do you good. Get you out the house.

He reckons he'll take me there and pick me up, just to make sure I'm not carrying on with someone else, Andrea laughed. I mean, can you believe it? I'm pregnant, with his child. And he still doesn't trust me. What else am I meant to do?

Sounds like he's insecure, Eileen said. Maybe he's not used to having a girlfriend with her own mind. You know what men are like.

It's not because he's a Paki, Andrea continued. He's had plenty of white girlfriends before. It's just, well, now he's got me he doesn't want to let go.

She stared up at the market ceiling.

I think he's frightened of losing me. His sister offered to pay for me to go to his family's village with him. It were a kind thought. That's a lot of money for her.

Why would you want to go there when your baby's due?

Think he wants to get married. He wanted me to go meet his Mam. I'm scared if I go I'll never come back.

Can't you get out of it?

Told him I'm not flying. No passport. Then he said he'd drive. It takes two weeks to get there overland.

Drive? Eileen shook her head.

I know. Imagine that. Being stuck with him in the car all

day for all that time. We'd kill each other before we even got there.

*

Andrea returned to Bowling Mill on split shifts throughout the week and often wore pan-stick around her eyes. Joan noticed that something was wrong and took her to one side on the late-shift break. They sat on the outdoor steps, overlooking the Bridge Tavern and talked about short time, the wage docks, Andrea's pregnancy and intimate details of post-childbirth stitches. Joan recalled the horrifying noises on labour wards when she had her daughter, Andrea said her mother advised her never to scream out and show herself up.

Is everything alright? You know, at home?

Joan leaned over and brushed Andrea's hair away, revealing a bruise that ran along her cheekbone.

I could swear you've got a black eye under there.

Andrea paused. She pulled her skirt down over the purple marks and turned to one side.

It's nothing. Just having a bit of a rough patch, that's all.

Look at your knees.

Getting used to it. You know, being belted. Dad used to bray me with a rotten hockey stick he kept behind the sofa. We all got a hiding off him. Just one of them things.

Joan leaned towards Andrea and chuckled.

Did you ever hit him back, you know, your old man?

No, but me Mam did. He used to kick off if I got caught slamming school. I mean, we all did it. There was this fella up there, Boardman, used to be a rugby player. He found me in Wibsey Park one day, messing about with the lads. Got a right thump when I went home.

But it's not the same, is it? You know, your Dad giving you a bollocking for slamming, and the person who's supposed to love you. The father of your child. I mean, it's not on.

The bell for the last shift rang in the background and echoed up the stairwell.

Fact of life, Andrea said. No point complaining.

She finished the last of her cigarette and stamped the end out on the metal grate, I'd be lying if I said it was all his fault. It takes two.

You'll have to be careful.

A few weeks back I didn't know where to hide ...

Andrea's voice drifted off as a pair of fighting starlings wrestled in the gutters above her. She unzipped her jacket and dusted down her cheesecloth shirt.

It's hard for me to walk away, because I don't want anyone to think I've failed ... but ... my family, they warned me not to go with him. I were being pig-headed and wanted to prove em wrong. Thought I knew best.

Joan held her hand out in front of her and pointed to the gold wedding ring on her finger.

You know, our Ron, she said. When things started out I thought he were the greatest thing that had ever happened to me. Before we got married he was sweet, I mean, a real romantic. Flowers and jewellery.

Can't imagine him being like that, Andrea said. He's got his good side but he can be a right miserable bastard.

Don't I know it.

Joan cackled with a raspy smoker's cough and cleared her throat.

But it wasn't until we lived together that I really saw what he were like. And by that time I'd had Julie and I couldn't leave.

They listened to the whirr of the looms that started moving on the floor behind them as the alarm bell rang for the last shift.

One night he chucked me down the stairs, Joan said. He'd been out on the tiles. Started riving at me, I were asleep.

What did you do about it?

Oh, you know. Same as you. Just tried to deal with it. Pride before fall an all that. I tolerated him. And now, well, he's older and much quieter. But sometimes, at night, I look at him and I still remember what he did. Some nights I still think about putting a pillow over his head. I just don't have the balls to do it.

*

So quiet in here. This cold house. Too far from home. My baby, you will soon be here. I don't know if you are a boy or girl. I don't care either way. But I want you to come soon. It hurts to breathe and I have to get up to pee in the night. Your Dad shouts at me for waking him up. I creep along the floorboards trying not to squeak them in the pitch black.

I hope you haven't heard the arguments in there.

I hope that you are born happy.

I hope that people aren't cruel to you for being half-caste.

I know you will be beautiful.

I cannot wait to take you into town in a pushchair in the bonnets your Gran Alma knitted. She has given me blankets and muslin cloth. My breasts are sore, they hurt when I touch them. My belly feels round but not so big that I can't put my shoes on. The midwife said I am carrying you towards my back so you might be a girl. I am wishing for an easy birth. The last month I have sat up writing every night to you. I clear the ashes out of the fire, light the small pieces of coal and lift up my jumper, let the warmth in.

I feel you kick and I know you can feel the fire too.

You will be my friend.

I will always love you.

*

Tick tock. Tick tock. Tick. Andrea listened to the hands on her bedside clock waiting for the baby to stir again. Only a few months had passed since the birth of Lorraine. She was born under a full pink moon. Spring was late and the daffodils had only just pushed their heads through the soil. It rained all day and as the nurses fed her with gas and air Lorraine's head pushed through onto the hospital bed. Jet black hair, long eyelashes and healthy lungs. The midwife cut the umbilical cord and slopped the baby onto her breast. Blood and mucus and overwhelming love.

For the first few weeks she forgot about everything that happened before. Nature erased her memory. Yousaf helped feed her between shifts and Shaffi bought toys for her cot; a fluffy rabbit, a lamb with a patterned dress, and a spotted dog with a moving head that played Brahms' *Lullaby* – the only way to get her to sleep. Every two hours she cried for a feed, and Andrea heated up her milk in the kitchen downstairs and rocked her by the back kitchen window. She rubbed cream into her cradle cap through her thick hair and traced her fingers over the fontanelle. Alma visited once a week, cooked her dinner and showed her how to wind when the baby cried.

Even when Lorraine slept insomnia kept Andrea awake. She often walked in the middle of the night to clear her head, to help the stitches heal. That was the quietest time. Peel Park was only a stone's throw from the house and on nights when Yousaf had finished a double-shift she knew he'd be spark out when his head hit the bed. She fed Lorraine, put her in the cot next to the mattress, and crept downstairs.

Andrea opened the back door quietly and tiptoed past the coal house, out of the yard and towards the street. Across the city she could see tops of the hills at Thornton, the lights twinkling at her. The Beacon was still there, in the distance. And sometimes, if she was feeling brave she'd jump into Undercliffe

Cemetery, the Highgate of the North. It was overgrown and ivy strangled the statues and columns. She read entrance signs that explained how it was first built due to a lack of places to bury the dead. Before Undercliffe was created, Bradford's corpses were dumped in makeshift burial pits, some so over-crowded that bones poked through the soil.

She walked through grand avenues of blackened stones, angels, anchors, doves, masonic eyes, clasping hands and crumbling urns, behind them the unmarked graves of thou-sands of Bradford's forgotten poor. Monoliths marked bodies of success: William Sharp, Fishmonger. Zackheus Akeroyd, Wool Stapler. Iron Moulders and Shop Keepers. Cloth Traders and Merchants. Sachs, Sussmann, Schloss, Behrens. The great and good of Worstedopolis. No Dunbars in Undercliffe though, or none that she ever noticed.

Andrea sat by the Barlow tomb where a white marble figure of a sleeping woman, draped in cotton sheets, with a baby under her arm, covered the tomb's lid. Above her a headless crucifix hung in the recess. Each time she night-walked through Undercliffe she stopped and stroked her feet.

Just before dawn was the quietest and coldest time of day. Nobody walked the streets. The roads were empty. If it rained, even better. She preferred it wet. Sometimes she walked through woodland at Peel Park. It was easy to hide in the bushes and rest with the birds. Andrea made a seat of leaves and waited for sunrise to come. She stared at the moon reflected in the lake's water, and traced the outline of her own face, her scars and pockmarks hidden by shadows. In the drizzling glow of the city lights she watched vixens skulk behind overflowing bins, pulling chicken carcasses from abandoned boxes, a hunger in their bellies.

When the time was right she'd make her move.

*

It's been getting worse. Lorraine won't stop crying and Yousaf is getting more angry. He keeps hitting me. I am worried the baby will grow up seeing me getting clouted by him.

Everything was alright before I moved up here. I don't know what's gone wrong. I think he has lost patience. It is time to go.

I am trapped. I miss Buttershaw. It's the only place where I feel safe.

I am frightened. I need somewhere where I can hide. Don't want to ring the police. My face is half-blue this morning and my lip is scabbed over. Yousaf told me the next time I won't be so lucky. I am confused. I love him but he hurts me. But I hate him too. I don't know what to do for the best.

He said if I go back to Buttershaw he will find me and drag me across the Arbor by my hair.

Sometimes I go to sleep and worry that I'll never wake up. He even chases me in my dreams.

The good thing is that I have £17 maternity allowance for eighteen weeks so that will keep me going.

I have kept the maternity grant hidden. It is £25.

I don't know how long I can last.

When Andrea's letter arrived at Eileen's house she read it three times and her hands began to shake.

After a few words with her neighbour who worked at the community centre Eileen walked to the phone box and called a social worker to ask for help. She had helped another woman, Marie, who had been beaten by her husband. Marie went to a refuge with her children. Then Leeds Council gave her a flat on Halton Moor and her husband never found her. He hung himself in the garage when he realised she wasn't coming back.

The wind blew through the broken glass of the phone box as Eileen scrabbled around for her last change. The concrete floor stank of old urine and a queue began to form outside as people checked their watches and tutted as she rang and re-rang until the phone was answered.

It's my friend, Eileen said. Needs help. I don't know what to do. Or how to get her out of there.

The social worker listened and made notes as Eileen spoke.

There's a new refuge on the edges of Keighley that has just been set up, she replied. I can't tell you where it is, but I can see if there's some space for her. It's for women only and it's essential that nobody finds out the address. She'll be safe there.

I'm not leaving her on her own. He'll find her and he'll kill her. Sorry. One moment . . . *what are you fucking looking at?*

She banged on the glass as a woman at the front of the queue folded her arms and peered in.

Everything OK?

The social worker waited as the phone swung from the receiver.

Yes. Nosy cow. She can do one.

Eileen lit a cigarette and continued.

I'm worried if she's there with the baby then there's nobody else there to look out for her.

Well, what are you suggesting?

Think I'd like to come with her, if that's alright. Dunno if that's allowed. But I'll be there, just for a few weeks. Might try it on with her but he'll never get past me. I'll batter him.

The social worker paused.

I'll see what I can do, she said. Make a few calls. It's important that your friend knows she can call the police anytime. I'm here during the day, so give her my number.

Will do. Thanks. I mean it.

I know you do. You take care.

Eileen wrote to Andrea that afternoon. Her letter was burned in the fire before Yousaf came home. It contained instructions for Thursday. The day when everything would change.

It was a slow day. Andrea had cleaned the house and washed the baby's clothes. She fed Lorraine and smoked out of the back door as she listened to the wireless. Autumn was closing in. Yousaf would be home in the afternoon, after clocking off from the 6–2. She made sure that his bread and butter was on the table when he came in. Nothing was out of place.

When he walked through the front door she kept a low

profile. He sat down in the back room and drank a mug of tea. She asked him how work was and he grumbled about Ali.

The doorbell rang at 3.30 on the dot.

Only Yousaf could answer the door, another one of his rules. Andrea bundled Lorraine into her cot.

The door rattled again. Andrea stood up and Yousaf pushed her down onto the chair.

You're not going anywhere, he said.

Yes I fucking am, she replied.

Do as I say. Sit down.

Yousaf bellowed and pulled out the ropes behind the table. It was the same thing every day. He tied her up so she wouldn't escape. Andrea started to complain and tried to push herself off the chair. He slapped her in the face and wrapped up her arms in knots. He pulled out his handkerchief and tied it over her mouth, muffling her screams that echoed down the corridor.

The door continued to bang. Yousaf brushed himself down and shut the door behind him. A young man stood on the steps. He was dressed in dirty jeans, an old jumper, and was chewing gum.

I'm sorry to bother you mate, me car battery's just died. Have you got any jump leads?

Yousaf was at first reluctant to help but his eyes lit up when he saw the Escort with alloy wheels parked outside the house.

Alright, erm. Well, I can have a look, Yousaf pulled his shoes on and stepped outside.

Cheers mate, must have left me lights on. No-one else seems to be in. I've tried next door.

They'll be at work. Give me a moment. I'll dig some out the cellar.

He shut the door and walked inside the house. Andrea was banging her feet on the floor in the back room.

Will you fucking shut up? he shouted. You're making a noise and I'm trying to help someone.

She listened as he rummaged through the shelves downstairs and brought out his tool box. What Yousaf didn't know was that Eileen was waiting in the back yard and was already hiding in the kitchen doorway.

She knew that her brother would keep Yousaf busy for the next few minutes. Andrea had tipped her off about Yousaf's obsession with cars and Eileen's brother would keep him distracted for the next few minutes.

Nice motor you've got there, Yousaf said. How much did you pay for it?

About £300. Got a deal off Lumb Lane, he replied. Saw it in *Auto Trader*.

Looks in good nick.

Eileen's brother ran his hands along the body of the car, scratted his balls and flegged on the pavement.

Yeah, it is. It's top notch, he said. Were thinking about getting it re-sprayed. Look, there's a bit round the side, think it got scratched by a bike.

I know someone who does that. He lives quite close, could

sort you out. My friend has a garage over in Lister Lane. Just up towards the junction.

Yousaf pointed to the mark as Eileen's brother opened his bonnet.

Oh, I know where you mean. The one that does cheap MOTs.

Yousaf connected the leads into his car and opened the door. He started the ignition and turned the engine over. That's the one, he said. Very good deal.

Does he do yours?

Yeah, tell him Yousaf from Solar Cars sent you, he replied. Speak to Big Andy. He should sort you out.

Eileen's brother started the engine on his car and leaned out the window.

Ta mate, you've really helped me, he said. That's almost running now.

As the two men chatted outside Eileen walked through the kitchen doorway – praying to God, if there was a God, that the baby wouldn't cry. When she bundled Lorraine into a sports bag, the baby opened her eyes and gurgled. Eileen put the dummy in her mouth that Andrea had left in the cot. Her brother was laughing on the front step. She knew when he beeped his horn Yousaf would be on his way inside.

Andrea winked at Eileen from the chair as she unknotted her; it took what seemed like an age. She winced as the gag was untied from around her mouth. Her hands were turning blue from the rope.

Let's get out of here before he twigs on.

No handbag, no keys, no money, no clothes. Andrea gulped for air and ran out of the door, picked up Lorraine, her carrier bag full of notebooks, and ran down the back alley with Eileen.

The car horn beeped.

The girls hurtled towards the traffic on Killinghall Road knowing that in only a few seconds Yousaf would find his girlfriend and daughter gone. They ran so fast that the exhaust fumes from the lorries and cars burned the insides of their lungs, Eileen's brother waited at the lights in his Ford Escort.

Can't believe we just did that.

I know. Can't breathe.

Andrea bolted towards his car as the lorries began to move along the road.

You alright?

Never been better, she said.

The car doors were open.

They jumped into the back, and the baby began to scream.

*

Hermit Hole, Ingrow, at 102 Halifax Road was the location of the first Women's Aid refuge in Keighley. It was the perfect place to hide. The house's discreet position was far enough away from the council, police and social services to attract any attention. It was acquired by Airedale Women's Aid in 1979 by a group of women connected to radical feminism in West

Yorkshire. Formed from the foundations of Bradford Women's Aid, a group who ran a refuge in the city, it provided a safe place for women who were fleeing domestic violence. The new shelter, a small terraced house, was entirely self-supporting.

It was sparsely decorated with donated furniture, and a typical West Riding overdwelling. Another house was built beneath it into the steep hillside. During the day a series of support workers checked in with the residents and provided them with advice and supplies. The residents were expected to run the house on an evening. It didn't matter how full the house was, shelter was always provided. Those were the rules. Women who had left their homes, sometimes with their children, stayed for as long as they needed to be there. It was run on a purely voluntary basis. The women who lived in the refuge were completely anonymous to the outside world.

The refuge's very first residents were two young women with barely any possessions from the Buttershaw Estate. The taller of the two, Eileen, had a young son. She told the refuge workers she was escaping her boyfriend who had beaten her. The smaller of the women, Andrea, spoke few words but said she was there to keep her friend company. She had a baby in her arms, a hold-all, and a carrier bag full of notepads. Her face had the ravaged look of a girl who had seen too much in her short life. It was a look that many women had at domestic violence refuges; eighteen going on forty.

Andrea hadn't told her family where she was staying, but wrote regular letters to Alma, telling her that she was alive and

Lorraine was keeping well. Eighteen years old and in hiding. No possessions apart from her daughter and notepads in the corner of the room that she looked at every day. She couldn't understand why she kept them. Winter clothes, toiletries, handbag, ID – all of those things would have been far more useful.

During the day she stayed inside the house, smoked cigarettes and watched television as the stench of cooking from the kitchen in the house below rose through the floorboards; reheated cabbage, jugged hare, fried bread in lard, fish on a Friday.

The support worker, Claire, visited every day. She brought food and newspapers with headlines about Prince Charles, Mrs Thatcher and the Yorkshire Ripper.

Oh dear, Claire said. It looks as though another poor woman has gone missing.

We know someone who he attacked, she lives near us. Maureen. Well, she reckons it were him.

Claire put her bag down in the kitchen and put two bottles of milk into the fridge.

Andrea uncrossed her legs and picked Lorraine up, putting her on her knee.

She'd been at Mecca, dancing. It were late, she said. There were a man outside in a car and she was drunk ... so she got in ...

Eileen walked into the kitchen and interrupted.

He pulled over near the railway lines to let her have a piss and when she crouched in the building rubble he bashed her with a brick.

Claire took a deep breath.

What an ordeal.

Pair of Alsatians who lived in a caravan started barking and scared him off, Andrea continued. She has deep holes in her head. Shows everyone the scars when she gets rat-arsed.

Eileen and Andrea started chuckling.

We shouldn't laugh, but what else are you supposed to do?

It is, what we call in the trade, gallows humour, Claire replied.

And what trade's that, then?

I'm actually part of a theatre group. That's my main job. Just volunteering here.

Claire laughed and pushed a ginger biscuit into her mouth.

Sorry, I'm stealing your food, she said. Hungry and pregnant.

Andrea paused, and began to speak slowly.

When you say theatre, do you write plays or are you an actress?

Some performance, yes. Mostly writing, and directing. A bit of everything. Have you been to the theatre before?

Oh no, apart from school, Andrea replied. I'd like to go, one day.

I work for a group based in Bradford and put on small productions around the area, community groups, that sort of thing. And, we work with quite a few female writers. I guess that's what I'm interested in.

Andrea's ears pricked up.

I write plays, she said.

Claire leaned back into the chair. Really. Tell me about what you write? You might be the first person I've met in a refuge who has written a play.

Did this play at school. My teachers thought it were good. They said I should write more.

Andrea boiled a kettle on the stove and started wiping the sides down, rinsed out the cloth and laid it in a neat fold over the taps.

And have you? Claire asked.

No, but I've got it upstairs. Only thing I kept.

Andrea pointed above her head.

Would you like to show it to me? Claire replied. I can read it if you want? Only if you want, of course.

Yeah, Andrea said. I'd like that.

Andrea ran upstairs and brought down a pile of paper covered in green biro, each page filled with scrawled teenager bubble writing.

This one, here. It's called *The Arbor*. My teacher sent it to YTV. It got turned down but the letter said I should keep writing. So I did.

Have you written anything else since then? Claire asked.

Just notes. Bits of conversations I've heard. It's all stuff I've seen happen. None of it fits together though . . .

Andrea's notepads were laid on the table. There were six in total. Claire could see that the dialogue had no strict form, but there were plenty of ideas.

I've never shown this to anyone. It's a bit like a diary. I've kept it over the past few years.

Listen, I might be able to help you, Claire said. I have friends who work in theatre. They could look at this, give you some advice.

Andrea shuffled the papers into a pile.

Maybe, she said.

You know Jalna, who helped you get this place?

Yeah.

Well, she has a friend in London who works with young writers. If you want, I can send these to her?

Claire leaned over to Eileen's son, Jamie, who ran into the kitchen pushing a toy train.

It would be a shame not to, she said.

Suppose there's nowt to lose.

Andrea drank the last of her tea and placed the cracked mug on the Formica top.

But I need em back, swear on your life you won't lose em.

I'll do my best, Claire replied. Do you think you can write a short note, explaining what they are?

Saying what?

Just a bit about yourself. Who you are. What you have written about. Maybe something about *The Arbor*, what it was based on.

I've no pen or paper.

That's alright. I'll go to the shop for you.

Claire picked up her car keys and walked out of the front door.

Have a think about what you might say, she said.

I'll be back in five minutes.

When Claire finally left the refuge that evening she drove straight to Jalna's house. She unpacked the papers and the two women read through Andrea's writing.

Jalna served two bowls of daal and chapatis onto the table and pulled out the opening page.

I'm not a dramatist, she said. This should go to Liane.

She's got a raw energy, Claire replied. I don't know what exactly. It's rough but there's talent here. Some of this . . .

She traced her fingers along the lines.

These lines are *smart*. She's a bright girl. It's quite, well, there are more than a few similarities with Brecht. Waterhouse perhaps.

High praise.

I'm sure Liane will see it. It needs work, but the shape is there. She has a good ear for speech and dialogue, this is already quite accomplished.

Perhaps I'll call Liane before I post it off? She's producing at the BBC right now; think she's working on that Christopher Logue poem.

Oh, I didn't know that. *War Music?*

Yes, the Homer one. I have no idea how they'll present it for radio.

Plenty of swagger, Claire replied.

Certainly. But it's nothing Liane can't handle. I do recall that she's still working on some young writers' scheme at the Court. She's open to suggestions as a rule . . .

Jalna bundled the notebooks into an envelope and included Andrea's letter.

A few weeks after the package had been sent to London, it arrived back at the refuge with a cover note. Andrea ran upstairs and threw the package onto the bed. Her hands shook as she tore at the envelope. She took a deep breath and started to read the letter.

Then she read it again.

It was written in fountain pen ink.

Dear Andrea

Thank you for sending me your notebooks. It was fascinating to read them.

What you have sent to me isn't quite like a play yet but you have written dialogue like you've heard it in your head. It reads more like a novel. Your characters are written in prose but there is so much dialogue here, that it is obviously a play.

Your writing is compelling and if you don't mind I would like to show some of it to Max, the Artistic Director at the Royal Court Theatre in London. There is great potential in what you have written. Although it is rough I can see how this patchwork of recollections and scenes could be drafted into a formal play.

I work as a freelance producer for the BBC at Langham Place but I have recently been working with the Royal Court as they have asked me to do a whole series on Children's Theatre. I am involved with working with young people and developing plays and I could help turn your notes into a script, if you are interested of course?

Once the lines have been condensed, and the scenes stitched together with some formal structuring I believe that The Arbor could be perfect for the radical pulse of the Royal Court. They are particularly interested in young female writers right now, and you might be just what they are looking for.

Yours sincerely

Liane

Andrea leaned back against the woodchip wall and stretched her arms as Lorraine pushed a rattle into her mouth. The orange headlights from a traffic jam outside the house shone through the nets onto her face.

At last, she said. Knew it had to come right in the end.

Lorraine rolled over onto her belly, kicked off her knitted boots and started to crawl across the faded carpet.

4

Red Mist

The front door of the refuge looked out onto the main road. Its outdoor windows were coated in diesel soot and the living room had an open fire. Once a week a delivery truck pulled up outside with a coal sack for the house. Aside from the occasional door-to-door salesman, or Jehovah's Witnesses peddling the apocalypse, the house was inconspicuous to the street and received few visitors.

What little money Andrea had saved from working in the mill had been spent on baby clothes for Lorraine, a second-hand fold out pushchair and food for her and Eileen. The social paid out her maternity benefit, but there was barely enough left at the end of each week.

If the weather wasn't tipping it down she risked walking into town at dusk, down the steep hill and along the cobbled back streets, past the black-faced Heber Street church where she often stopped and peered through the glass at the preacher who spoke to spirits in tongues of the long-dead.

She replayed the previous months in her mind and relived the scenes. She saw his face in every corner. Even with her hat, winter coat and boots on, she wondered if someone might recognise her. It was miles away from home, but every white car could be his.

This was what love and hate felt like.

His body, his face, equally repulsed and attracted her. Violence was the only way Yousaf knew how to keep her. Paranoia and jealousy festered. Their child a daily reminder of him.

His face in her daughter's. His hands around her neck. His tongue in her mouth. Her blood on his shirt.

Red mist.

Red mist.

Red mist.

Yousaf couldn't read, but she continued to send him notes via Alma, who posted them from Shelf Top. Shaffi read the postcards for him; she knew he would try to find her.

The messages were short. She asked if he could send money to Brafferton Arbor for the baby. He often waited in his car around Buttershaw, watching, waiting for her to appear. Alma wouldn't budge and knew what he wanted; she'd had a lifetime of dealing with difficult men. Yousaf's threats didn't scare her; her blood and bones were made of sterner stuff. He banged

and shouted outside Alma's house until David chased him off
with a plank of wood.

*

*Drowsy afternoons. The springs poke through the mattress. Four
blankets. The streetlamp switches on in the afternoon. It is dark
down here. I can hear the steam train going past round the back. It
covers the valley with even more smoke.*

*Lorraine keeps crying, she is teething. Her cheeks are bright red.
District Nurse came to check on her this week. Told me I had to
bath her in the morning, but mum said I should do it just before
bed, that way she'll sleep better. I only take notice of her. She's
had eight, knows more about it than anyone else. We turned out
alright.*

*She showed me a trick, how to put Calpol on the spoon and dip
the dummy in, that way she'll take it without noticing. Mum says
it's all about the tricks, and I'll learn that sooner or later.*

*Looked at myself in the mirror for the first time in months. Could
barely bring myself to look at my face this time last week. It was
covered in bruises, purple round my left eye. But now they've almost
gone. Just the odd scratch mark and scars on my arm. My hair is
frizzy, need new clothes. Been wearing Sally Army handouts for as
long as I can remember.*

*It's eleven miles to Buttershaw, Eileen checked with her brother
who does deliveries round here. Keep thinking about walking it,
when the weather gets better. Still don't feel safe, but it's better than*

it was. *Claire and Jalna treat me well. They talk to me about theatre and writing. They left me a bag of scripts to read for when I'm not too tired. Read* It's a Madhouse *and* A Taste of Honey *in front of the fire, still can't get on with Shakespeare.*

We have started smoking outside. We keep the front door half-open and take the piss out of the neighbours. Mrs Bacon is the woman next door who smells of pork fat. Alf Roberts is the woman who lives across the road and scrubs her front step every morning in a pinafore.

There's another neighbour called Mick who has a red Vauxhall and always parks outside our front door. He's almost forty and dyes his hair. He always shouts MORNING GIRLS! when we stare at him from the house. He is married, and leaves for work with his tool box every day. His missus minds the children. She has a mouth like a cat's arse. He says he spends as little time with her as possible.

He wears tight trousers and aftershave. His shirt is unbuttoned down to the chest and he whistles when he walks past the house. Thinks he's Barry Gibb. His hair is thinning on top, we reckon he colours it with a spray. When everything was quiet the other night he stopped outside the door and knocked, I invited him in and he sat down on the sofa. We sat either side of him, and he laughed at our jokes as we drank mugs of tea.

Mick spread his legs apart, rattled his bracelet and said So, what's a lovely-looking pair like you doing living round here? Fancy a trip to Baildon Moor sometime?

*

Up a steep hill, a stone's throw from the refuge, Halifax Road led up to the moor tops and eventually down into Bradford. The fields were lined with stone walls that tumbled into the sodden peat and heather lands covered the wind-whipped peaks of West Riding.

In the middle of summer the weather was harsh and often shifted within a matter of minutes from bright sunshine into torrential rain. There was no place to hide. Even the hardiest sheep were taken down from the tops in winter and clustered in groups in the corner of fields when bitter squalls lashed over gateposts.

Gingerbread Clough, Catstones Moor, Lingbob, Denholme Clough, Mickle Moss, Blackshaw Beck and Soaper Lane. Blackened terraces silhouetted across hilltops where the outline of outdoor privies and crooked walls formed jagged shapes on the horizon. Smoking steeples reached towards the clouds and dense fog slowly drifted along the streets.

Cathedrals of industry, factories and mills, their lights flickered in the night. Cobbled lanes shone with black ice, steam rose from the grates.

Andrea bundled Lorraine into her pushchair and walked through Ingrow, towards Denholme as the weather battered their cheeks. She pushed until she could barely breathe. Her fingers frozen by the cold. It took almost two hours to walk up the hill, past rows of barbed wire with tufts of sheep-down, the crumbling stone walls, and acres of bleached grass that stretched as far as the eye could see. By the time she reached Keelham she sat by the roadside and fed Lorraine a bottle in the shelter of a gnarled hawthorn tree. A van pulled up a few minutes later.

A man wearing overalls and steel cap boots walked towards her.

Now then, he said.

He had a dark beard and thick black hair.

Do you know the route to Hipperholme? I've been driving around for ages . . .

Erm. Keep going this way, back on the main road.

Andrea shuffled away from him.

It'll be signposted.

Bit cold to be out, he said. Where you heading?

Bradford. It's not far.

Her pram rattled in the wind and the rain began to sheet around them.

Look love, it's terrible weather. Can't I give you a lift?

The man pointed to his van. The light was on in the cabin.

No, she replied. I'll be reet. Not far to the bus stop now. Could do with the fresh air.

The man reached towards Lorraine, Andrea flinched.

It's alright, he said. Only trying to be nice.

That's what they all say, she replied.

Andrea bundled Lorraine into the pushchair and began to walk away.

The man sat back behind his wheel and followed her along the road with his window down.

You're safer in here than out there, he said. I can run you back home. Lass like you shouldn't be up here wandering.

Already told you, she replied. Don't need a lift. Don't need any help. I'm alright as I am.

When she arrived on the estate that evening Andrea was greeted by packs of stray dogs that jumped up at her and chased her down the street. One had the head of a collie, the trunk of an Alsatian and legs of a terrier. Frankenstein dogs that howled and fucked and fought in the middle of the road.

One of the things she didn't miss about Buttershaw was the dogs. Or the noisy Irish neighbours who shouted and bawled from their balcony. But she missed her family, and even her Dad, in a funny way.

Her little sister Jeanette ran down the path to meet her as she walked up the garden path and locked the wheels of the pushchair. Lorraine had slept most of the way, and started to wriggle as they approached the house. Andrea hadn't been home in months. She dried herself off and pulled an envelope from her bag.

Hello stranger. My, you've grown.

Alma bent down and picked Lorraine up. What a bonny bairn. Can't believe how big she is.

Andrea held out her hands.

My fingers are blue. It's freezing out there, thought I was going to die.

It's not that bad, Alma said. I've seen far worse. When you were her age it was that cold the trees cracked.

I've some news . . . can't get me head around it. An actual theatre, somewhere in London, is, more or less, interested in me. You know that script that I did at school? Well, I worked on it a bit and the women at the refuge posted it off.

Are you getting paid for it? Alma asked.

Andrea paused and read through the letter.

I think so, yes.

Well, that's grand.

She hugged the baby and nodded at Andrea.

We're very proud of you.

Probably won't happen. They'll change their minds. But, all the same, they think my writing is good.

Andrea sat down next to the glowing embers of an Irish fire and read Liane's letter aloud.

Well, maybe you could make a name for yourself, Alma said. You could write for *Coronation Street*. Hey, you could take us all abroad. Wouldn't that be fun.

Never thought I'd be a writer. Just imagined it in my head. Some bloke from London wants to come and see me. A director ...

Alma started folding the piles of washing, shook out the creases in the shirts and shouted through from the kitchen.

You've walked all the way up that hill from Haworth, can see colour in your face, she said. You're not showing it but I know you must be right chuffed with yourself.

I am, Mam, she smiled. They say it's going to be put on in London. I've never been further than Leeds.

*

Max made the journey north in November when Andrea was still living at the refuge. It was before the trouble started with Mick. Andrea's case workers decided she should meet Max in a neutral space, a supervised environment where she felt safe. Jalna suggested that her home, on Ivybank Lane in Haworth, could be used.

The house was situated in a terrace on an old track with deep ruts. Max drove up to the town, making the five-hour trip up the M1 from Gloucester Crescent, his home in London which overlooked Regent's Park. He parked in the town centre and walked up to Jalna's house, where she made him tea and told him about the refuge and the women they helped.

Andrea arrived shortly afterwards and sat in the corner of the living room, with Lorraine in her pushchair. Max, in his theatrical manner, shook her hand.

Hello Andrea, he boomed. How marvellous to finally meet you. It really is an honour.

Andrea pulled her cold palms from his hot grip. His hands were smooth and soft, like a woman's. She sat down in the corner of the room and placed Lorraine's pushchair in the hall.

Claire offered to keep an eye on her, picked her up and pointed outside to the street.

There's a cat, she said. Can you see it?

Max crossed his legs and placed a leather-bound diary on the coffee table.

Well, I've read a draft of your play. May I say how impressed I am by your writing. Did it take long to create?

No, Andrea said and stared at the floor.

Have you been to London before? He tucked his long curly hair behind his ears and rolled the ends of his thick handlebar moustache between his fingers.

No. Never been anywhere.

We'd very much like to offer you an opportunity to come to the Royal Court. Writers are incredibly important to us, and we endeavour to find the very best young playwrights in the country. I sincerely believe you are one of them. Does this sound of interest?

Dunno, she replied.

Andrea stared through the nets as a delivery van parked outside the house.

Will I get paid?

Of course, there is a fee for all writers. Not much, but enough to help develop your script. Our writers are at the core of our philosophy . . .

Oh, she interrupted. How much? What will I get?

That can all be sorted out by the office.

Max grinned and she noticed the signet ring on his left hand, glimmering in the afternoon light.

Now, I am curious to know, have you ever been to the theatre before?

No.

He nodded and wrote down a few words in tiny, neat handwriting.

That is interesting, he said.

How will I get the money? See, thing is, her voice started to rise. If you send it to Brafferton then me Dad'll spend it down the pub. You'll have to sort it with the Post Office. I don't have a bank account.

That can be arranged. More importantly though, I'd like to invite you down to London to start work on *The Arbor*. It really is one of the best scripts I've seen by a young writer in a long time. You have an extraordinary gift for dialogue, but it needs some work. A friend of mine who is a playwright read it and agreed that you have talent spilling over . . .

Max's news about the play wasn't met with enthusiasm, in fact, her stoicism unsettled him. Like many Yorkshire people Andrea didn't show excitement, good news was downplayed. It was almost an embarrassment.

Anyway, she replied. I've stuff to be getting on with. It's getting dark.

Oh . . .

Max stood up to say goodbye and Andrea turned away, picking up her coat and bag.

Andrea, you know I've driven quite a long way, I thought we might discuss the script further?

Baby needs feeding and I've shopping to get in.

Alright. Well, I'll write to you next week. We can get the details sorted out then.

Send me train tickets and I'll come to London, she said. Send me the money first.

*

On the roundabout of the Braithwaite Estate groups of young boys hung around the shop front, cadging cigarettes and throwing exploding pop bottles at passing cars. They already had the faces of old men, drinkers and robbers. Some acted with the confidence of their teenage brothers. Dressed in torn jeans and scraggy jumpers they bent over railings that overlooked the ring, the main roundabout on the estate where all the drama happened. The ringleader spat on the tarmac every few seconds and managed a long stringy greenie as soon as he had an audience.

On the grass verges around the shop, which were overgrown with skeletal dandelions and browning ragwort, empty beer cans piled up in windy corners with mounds of dog shit from local mutts. Andrea watched them when she caught the bus from the other side of the ring, and thought that there was barely any difference between Buttershaw and Braithwaite. Same houses, same problems, same families, same lack of money. No jobs, high crime, isolation, desperation, a steady diet of nothing.

To get to Alma's house she caught the bus into town, then a train to Bradford, and another bus to Buttershaw past the factories, mills, gasworks, scrap-yards and chimneys that faded into the city's smog. It sometimes took half a day to get there.

The estate looked out across the Worth Valley and was a two-mile walk uphill from Keighley town centre. In the winter, with a pushchair and a toddler, Andrea could barely manage to get the shopping in. She'd catch the 702 bus into town, and if she had any change, used the red phone box next to the bus stop to call the Royal Court.

Andrea moved in with Mick after it had all kicked off at the refuge. There was no end of trouble. Eileen watched the kids, and Mick drove Andrea up onto Baildon Moor. They'd listen to a loud car tape on the way home, and the next day, Andrea would offer to watch the children again. It seemed like the perfect arrangement until one night he was seen in the Bierkeller, doing the conga with Andrea and Eileen on the dancefloor. Word soon got out and the front door was almost kicked through.

It was bad news for the refuge; they prided themselves on discretion. The new residents had brought trouble to the neighbourhood. The refuge workers were horrified that Mick had taken advantage. He had been spotted climbing in through the front window one night, after the house had been locked up and had shouted Andrea's name from the pavement, howling like a drunken Romeo in his tight white pants.

There was no telephone in the new flat on Braithwaite, on the fifth floor of Littondale House, a block of flats on Whinfield Drive. Mick rented it off the council. It was the cheapest place he could find. It had a three bar fire that they huddled around at night, burning the curlies on their legs when they sat too close.

It was close to the top of the hill of the estate and had green and grey wallpaper in psychedelic swirls, making it feel even darker when the sun clouded over. The hallway had Anaglypta walls and an Artex ceiling. The skirting boards were painted dark brown and the bathroom was orange and brown. Each wall had a pattern, every window had nets. At least Lorraine had her own room. The refuge workers warned her about Mick, but nothing anyone said would make her stay away from him.

*

Sat on the train on my way to King's Cross. It was only Christmas a few weeks back. Feels like I've been living in the dark all winter. The sun is out today. It's the first time I've been this far anywhere on my own. Rob sent me tickets from the Court and here I am, at a table, looking out over the flooded fields. I have just passed the cooling towers and I can see the colliers bringing coal out of the pits. Big black slag heaps run alongside the railway line.

Mam is looking after Lorraine, she's up on her feet now, pulling sugar pots from table tops.

I am meeting Liane when I get off the train, she said I can stay at her house in north London.

My tummy is fluttering so much that I can't think about eating and all I can do is drink beer. I've a four-pack in my holdall and although it's only morning I've already had two. Had the shits first thing. Must be nervous. At least I can smoke in here.

When I rang the Court last week everyone sounded posh. They kept asking me to repeat myself, to talk slowly. Must sound like I'm talking another language. Max said they see something special in me, but what that is I don't even know myself.

London looks big and frightening on the television, but at least I'll get chance to see Leicester Square and Big Ben, Madame Tussauds and Buckingham Palace. Can't wait to tell Eileen about it.

So, almost here.

Fell asleep for a bit, holding my pen.

Spilt my can on the table.

It's sticky.

Can see signs for Finsbury Park and the train guard says we're almost here. I wound the window down to stop feeling sick and stuck my head out like a dog in a backseat of a car. People look like ants on the street. Thousands of buildings and sirens going off.

Think I'm excited but I won't let them know that.

*

Liane met Andrea off the train at King's Cross, a large Victorian station that looked like the old Bradford one before the council demolished it. Andrea stepped off the train and took her coat off.

God, it's a bit hot down here, isn't it? she said.

Welcome to London, Liane replied. I hope you enjoy your time here. I'll take you on the Underground over to my office at Broadcasting House. We'll have a look at your writing when we get there and then we'll have fish and chips.

Andrea had arranged to spend time with Liane. They agreed

to work during the day to create a draft script of *The Arbor* in Liane's office where together they'd plot out the various scenes and make it look like a play. After tea they'd talk about the meeting which was happening the next day at the Royal Court, and Andrea would sleep on the sofa. Liane's two sons lived with her; they would be up early for school the next day.

When they arrived at Langham Place, Liane pointed up to the building.

This is the home of the BBC, she said. I'm going to take you on a tour.

I've seen this on the telly before, Andrea said. It looks like summat from a film.

See that wall, over there, it has a statue on the side, called a relief. That one is Prospero and Ariel, have you ever heard of *The Tempest*?

Uhm, no.

Andrea stared up at the stonework and blew her nose in a handkerchief. She began to cough.

It's a bit fumey down here, she said. Me hankie's black.

Liane leaned over and shouted at the Hackney Cabs that beeped on the road behind them.

It's a play by Shakespeare. These two are characters, she said. An artist called Eric Gill made it. You see, Prospero was a magician and Ariel is the spirit of the air, which in radio waves means travel.

So, an old man with a beard groping a boy with no clothes on, Andrea said. Can we go in yet?

Yes, she replied. But you know why I've shown you this?

Hmmm. Cos it's radio?

Indeed. And because my office is just behind it.

They entered the building, signed in, and walked past various offices on the third floor.

Liane gave Andrea a pen and paper, and she sat on a desk in the corner of the editing suite reading her notes. It was a noisy room, with editors talking and dialogue being chopped up and rewound on spools. Music was cut into the edits, and machines blipped and stuttered throughout the afternoon. This was nothing compared to the noise Andrea encountered at home or at the mill. She tuned her ears out of the chaos and worked on the lines.

Andrea drank cups of tea and scribbled notes. Some of the other editors came in and said hello to her. Their voices sounded posh. But what she first thought would be a frightening experience wasn't one at all. It was almost as though she was made for it. The words in her head flowed out. Having the time to write her thoughts down was a luxury. Liane helped her with the page layouts and after a few hours a script was created on a notepad that she took to the Court the following day.

When they arrived at Liane's flat in Hampstead she was exhausted. The tree-lined avenue had houses with white-washed steps leading up to them and grand doorways with potted plants and tidy front gardens outside. Liane's flat was elegantly decorated. Each room had bookshelves and leaves of exotic plants tumbled from windowsills. Bright pictures hung on the walls and glassware glistened from the mantelpiece. She daren't touch a thing.

Outside, the streets were full of houses with stained-glass front doors, and even if they had shabby windows, they looked like palaces compared to Buttershaw.

Where are the estates around here? Andrea asked as she shovelled a fork of chips into her mouth. Does all of London look like this?

*

Andrea arrived at the Court with a pile of notes under her arm and her holdall in the other. Her jacket was draped over her shoulders, her face was pouring with perspiration. She sat on a bench overlooking the theatre on Sloane Square and straightened her trousers where the seam had dropped. A piece of Sellotape hung from the ankle, damp with the heat of London. Andrea tugged it away from the fabric, rolled it into a ball and flicked it at a woman who walked past in an expensive camel coat.

Andrea watched the building for a few minutes to see if anybody left the theatre. A woman dressed in a boiler-suit left the side door, and Andrea walked across the eastern side of the square towards her. A sign reading Young People's Theatre was hung above a garage, and she walked up an old wooden staircase towards a room where she could hear voices. Two women were carrying boxes of newspaper cuttings down the stairs.

Hello, they shouted. Can we help you?

Andrea quickly ran down the stairs and onto the street, her face flushed with embarrassment.

One of the women, dressed in a bottle green sweater and high boots ran after her.

Wait, she grabbed her by the arm. Are you looking for someone?

Supposed to be meeting Max.

Oh. Right. Well, you'd better come with me. I'll take you in.

When they entered the theatre, the woman turned to her on the steps.

I'm Sophie, very glad to meet you, she said.

Sophie had a perfect upturned nose, glossy hair and a voice that bounced off the walls. Andrea walked behind her, with her eyes fixed on the carpet.

Andrea, she said. Dunbar. From Bradford.

It's a real pleasure to make your acquaintance, we've heard *so* much about you.

Andrea shrugged and put her hands in her pocket as the box office rang through for Max.

Yes . . . of course, Max . . . I'll do that . . . ten minutes? Fine.

She turned to Andrea.

Apparently Max is in a meeting, but he'll be down soon. I'll give you a quick tour of the building. You can leave your bags here, behind the desk.

Not leaving my bags anywhere, Andrea replied. I'll bring it meself.

How about the notepads? We can put them somewhere safe . . .

Safe enough wi me.

Okay, let's go downstairs.

You know the Court, it is so much *more* than a building. It is, a way of life, an attitude, a form of thinking . . .

Andrea walked slowly behind her down the darkened corridor.

It was built in 1888, Sophie said. With four storeys and Corinthian columns to the upper floor. We have an unreliable lighting system which places it at a high risk of fire. As you can see, it's quite antiquated. The seats are upholstered in velvet and provide some comfort to audiences during performances despite their incessant creaking.

Andrea sat down on a velvet seat and stared up at the stage.

Recently we had a dreadful storm and drains flooded the stalls, so we still have a few repairs to do. You can see the names of the donors on the back of the new seating. The dressing rooms aren't much better, and the office spaces are cramped. You can still see the water marks on the floor.

Was the floor covered in shit? Andrea said.

I believe so, yes. The mighty excrement of London's theatre community.

So is this where my play will be on?

No, you'll be upstairs. I'll take you up to the lighting box, the lights often move in performances when the trains run underneath. They shake the building's foundations.

There was an awkward silence.

I'll stay here, thanks, Andrea said.

Okay, she sighed. What else can I tell you? Well, this is where many great plays have first been performed. John Osborne's *Look Back in Anger*, for example. George Devine had put an advert in *The Stage*, asking for submissions of scripts. Osborne's play was selected. It opened to half-empty audiences and mostly dreadful reviews.

Sophie grinned and flicked her ponytail to one side.

Another one you might have heard of is Edward Bond's *Saved*?

Andrea shook her head.

It featured a scene in which a baby was stoned to death, and the play was denied a licence. You had to go through the censors back then. The Court refused and after that the law was changed. It was quite an important play in many respects.

Can we go see the Theatre Upstairs?

Most certainly, Sophie replied. It used to be a nightclub owned by Clement Freud. You know the Freuds, of course? This is where the Young Writers' Festival was founded and most of our young writers start out here.

Andrea walked into the compact space with around sixty seats pointing towards a small raised stage.

It's a bit pokey, she said. Thought it'd be downstairs.

Sophie blurted a deep laugh.

Oh goodness, no! Whatever gave you that idea? Only the biggest names down there.

A voice boomed from the stairwell and Max's shadow appeared up the steps, crouching towards the main light before his face peeked around the door frame.

You made it, he said.

About bloody time, Andrea replied. Losing the will to live, up here.

I've brought you some tea.

Max sat down beside her and put a tray on the floor. Hot water spilled from the pot and dripped over the edge.

So, Nicholas Wright started all this, he said. Our young writers meet here regularly, and come from all over London to this space. Lenka Janiurek's *In the Blood* was performed here a couple of years ago, I'd very much like you to read her work.

Andrea remained silent.

Your play will be performed in here on the 11th of March. So that's not too far off.

So why am I here now? she replied. I've done some writing with Liane, got it typed up yesterday.

We have a long way to go yet. You'll get to sit in on rehearsals, watch the play as it's being developed, and change it when required. There will be an awful lot of work for you to do as a writer throughout this period.

Andrea handed the typed notes to Max and he began to underline, cross out and circle the lines with his pencil.

This is just the beginning, he said. I do hope you like it here.

5

Muck or Nettles

A film crew came up from London last week. They met me outside Littondale and filmed inside the flat. Had to clean it from top to bottom. Mick was out. They followed me walking around the estate with Lorraine in her pushchair. Before that they made me put her jacket on three times until the light was right.

A man called Nigel from the BBC interviewed me. He kept asking what life was like on a Yorkshire council estate, and what people thought about me writing about them. It was hard to answer. I hadn't really thought about it. The baby kept crying and we had to do extra takes. It was raining. A wardrobe woman gave me a blow-dry beforehand but it frizzed out when the wind hit it. Bet I look a right state when it's on.

They talked to me about the play and my life. Can't understand what's so interesting about it, but Max seemed to think I should do the programme, so I did. The camera filmed me feeding Lorraine, then walking to the bus stop and getting onto the train at Keighley. They didn't even help me with the pushchair, had to fold it up myself. People in town were sniggering and talking under their breath when we walked past. They thought I couldn't hear them. Who does she think she is they said. Stuck up cow. Why are the BBC filming her, what a tramp. I kept my head down and carried on walking.

I wore my best cotton jacket and a knee-length skirt. They filmed me looking out of the train through the grubby glass. They said they wanted to catch me when the mills and steeples were in the background. The camera rolled when we passed the back-to-backs.

We got off the train and went to Impact. Lee let them film me at my desk and they asked about the Youth Opportunities Scheme. I told them about the refuge and how they had offered me a job there writing letters, filing scripts and helping with community plays in Bradford. That was alright. But then they kept going on about Buttershaw, what it was like being an unmarried mother, and what I thought about abortion. Told them I didn't have many friends since having a baby, too busy. Kept saying keep myself to myself. Knock about with the lasses at work. But don't go on nights out. Just stay in. Best way to be.

Some neighbours might be shocked by what I wrote. But I didn't even think of that until the cameras were going. But whatever I write it has to be my story. So at least I have the chance to say it. As I told them, you write what's said. You don't lie. Or say it didn't happen when it did all the time . . .

*

107

Eileen walked slowly up the hill towards Littondale House, past the houses and flats that perched on steep verges facing south. The orange glow of Keighley illuminated the mills which manaufactured rolls of Fleur de Lys carpet and luxury rugs. Chimneys coughed their first fires into the air and double-deckers honked at workers who streamed out onto the streets after clocking off.

Rain bounced off the asphalt and flooded drains were blocked by fallen leaves. Lorries sprayed water onto Eileen's jeans. She shouted at drivers as they deliberately hit puddles at high speed. Her hair was soaking and rain dripped down the back of her neck, past her shoulders and into her underwear.

When she arrived at Andrea's flat the front doorbell was hanging off. She leaned over a fence, picked up a handful of gravel and threw it three floors up, only managing to hit the right window after various attempts. The window was steamed and curtains were drawn. She threw another, larger stone, and almost smashed the pane. Andrea's face appeared at the glass as she opened the rickety frame.

About bloody time! Been stuck down here for hours.

Do that again and I'll drop a bucket of water on you.

A keychain dropped onto the grass below.

Eileen ran up the stairwell and unlocked the sticking door; she pushed it forward into the pitch-black flat.

Bit dark in here, she said. Why's the light off? Sat in the dark. On your own.

Nowt's up. Out of money for the meter. So it's light or heat.

Andrea dropped a blanket onto Eileen's knees as they sat down in front of the fire.

Got soaked on the way up, Eileen said. And it's freezing. Took a day to get up here.

Stop exaggerating.

Well, maybe not a whole day.

Eileen rubbed her palms together and blew on them.

Juicy fag?

Go on, then.

Andrea pulled out a packet of cigarettes and leaned towards the bars of the gas fire. She pushed each one into the grate and sucked on them until they ignited.

Don't say I don't spoil you . . .

So, how've you been?

Andrea paused.

Bit shit to be honest.

Thought you'd be happy now you're famous. Mam said you came across well on the box.

Rehearsals looked alright, Mia and Jane, and Kathryn. They did a good job . . .

So, what's up?

Theatre sent me the newspaper cuttings after it's been on. They're in the kitchen, on the side.

Eileen walked across the room and picked up the envelope.

I can't bloody read them with the lights off, she said. Or with a Zippo. I'll go read em outside.

She walked into the corridor and held the articles up against the stairwell light which spat and dimmed as the bulb gave up the ghost. She read the headlines aloud.

A Divided Community, Nasty Brutish Bradford Life, Getting out of Buttershaw ... divided? What are they on about? Nasty? Brutish? Is that what they think of us?

They've been writing all this stuff about me since that programme were on. Haven't even seen the play. But they just keep going on about me being unmarried and living on an estate. They've writ some stuff about Buttershaw, her voice croaked. Mam reckons there's hell on with the neighbours.

Complaining neighbours? No change there, then. They've nowt else to do except nosy into other folk's business. Pay em no mind.

Andrea huddled behind Eileen in the doorway and read out an article from the *Guardian*.

Look at this one, she said. *Brafferton Arbor is the worst street on the worst estate in Bradford* ...

Well, they do have a point, Eileen laughed.

Don't fucking laugh, Andrea said. It's not funny. They go round writing that, then someone reads it and it lands on our doorstep. And besides, how do they know it's the worst street? Have they been to every single one? No. Have they bollocks.

Fair point, reckon there's streets like ours all over Leeds, I mean, even Mixenden's rougher than Buttershaw. Why should ours be worse than any others? That old trout down the road's been shouting her mouth off again.

What's she say this time?

That Buttershaw looked a tip on the telly. That it made her look bad.

Huh, Andrea chuntered. All about her as usual.

She said it looked dirty . . .

Some of it is. There's a few houses near the Crescent, people don't care. Leave their stuff everywhere. That's not my fault, is it? Only write about what I see. Here, have a mint.

Andrea put a Polo into her mouth and blew through the hole.

They'll forget about us by tomorrow, she said.

*

When BBC's *Arena* interviewed Alma, John Brian, and the rest of the family on the doorstep of 26 Brafferton Arbor the previous month, her father, his hair greased back, and a brown suit jacket, minus his false teeth, had beamed with pride.

ALMA: We don't all live here now. There were ten
    of us altogether, nine now.
INTERVIEWER: And have any of the other
    children written anything?
ALMA: No.
INTERVIEWER: So what do you feel about
    Andrea writing a play?
ALMA: I'm proud of her.
INTERVIEWER: Can I ask you, Mr Dunbar,

where do you think she gets her writing from?

JOHN BRIAN: Well, not from me, certainly. I don't know; it's just what she learned at school I should imagine.

INTERVIEWER: Have you read the play?

JOHN BRIAN: No, I haven't.

INTERVIEWER: Are you going to see it, in London?

JOHN BRIAN: No, but the wife is, and my daughter Pamela. I'm at home with the children.

INTERVIEWER: Mrs Dunbar, can I ask if you have read it?

ALMA: Oh, I've read it. It'll be summat different, won't it?

INTERVIEWER: Do you hope Andrea will go on to write more plays?

ALMA: Yes, I hope she'll make a success of herself.

Alma caught the train with Andrea to watch the opening night of *The Arbor* at the Young Writers' Festival in March, 1980. Before the preview, they had their photograph taken outside the theatre on Sloane Square. Alma's hair had been set for the occasion and she wore her best sandals and leather coat. Andrea wore her wool jacket and cotton trousers. A photographer gathered them together under a London plane tree, and told them he worked for the Press Association. Mother and daughter posed for the camera. The flash bounced off their cheeks.

You'll never guess what, they've asked me if I'd like to see the play on in the main theatre, big one, downstairs, Andrea said. Since it was on TV it's all sold out. So they've asked me to do another act.

Well done.

Alma beamed at the photographer, who shouted directions at them in the busy street.

Still to write it. Might do summat about Yousaf. What happened last year.

You be careful, Alma replied. I mean it. Don't push yourself too much. Know how tired you get.

Not like I'm on my feet all day, combing.

You're right there. Nowt more back-breaking than that. Covered in grease with headphones on, lugging baskets of worsted around.

They walked over the pelican crossing towards the front steps of the theatre. Andrea pointed to the illuminated signage that hung over the entrance.

See that sign, up there? My name's gonna be on it. Next to *Hamlet*. Honest, Max told me last night. My name in lights. For all of the city to see.

*

More to worry about than writing. Not on my list of priorities, but it should be. Hardly slept for a month. Thought it was meant to be easier than this. So here I am. Just gone three and I'm sat up writing. Piles of paper on the table. Letters to reply to. Max said I should let it all out through the characters.

When I write, I live through it again. Yousaf. The arguments. Getting pregnant. The refuge. Writing doesn't solve any problems. But at least I can control it. Not like when it happened.

Max keeps trying to call me, it never works out. Reversed charges last night from the phone box. He shouted at me for interrupting his rehearsal. Said I should have called when he'd arranged. That he had other things to worry about, not just me. Told him to fuck off, then he said you fuck off and all. In Dad's voice. I cracked up laughing and it was all alright.

He said the thing is about the Court, you can tell whoever you want to fuck off and they won't be offended. I said well that's alright as I'll be doing a lot of that this month. Then I told him about Mick, he said nothing's wasted and I should write it down before I forget. Told him how the windows had been put through after a fight with the neighbours. Oh goodie, he said. What's good about that? I said. You know exactly what I mean, he said. Told him I'd written a scene but I'm not sending it down because it's crap. That's what I like to hear, he said and hung up the phone.

Haven't seen Mick in two days. Went to the shop and never came back. Neighbours keep banging and playing music all day, all night. That song. Kiss You All Over. *If I hear it one more time I'll put my fist through the wall. That knobhead keeps playing it.*

I miss The Arbor.

Miss Mam.

Miss Pam, David, Kathy and Jean.

Want to sign off the dole.

Want enough money for the meter.

Want my own place.

Want to go back to Buttershaw.

Want a better life for Lorraine.

Either I write or go back to the mills.

There's no other way out.

*

Andrea stayed at Max's house on Gloucester Crescent throughout the week of rehearsals, and was joined by Eileen a few days later on her first trip to London. She met her at King's Cross and together they caught the Tube up to Camden Town. The journey had taken four hours already, and Eileen was exhausted by the heat and noise of the city. The Underground terrified Andrea. When she saw Eileen's silhouette bounding down the platform with her holdall bag and bottle of Blue Nun her face lit up.

Can't believe I'm here. So bloody chuffed to see you. Look at this place!

Not bad, Andrea replied. People have so much money. It's like another world.

Eileen hadn't travelled on the Underground before, and was

taken aback at the speed of the trains as they flew past her face towards the north of the city.

We'd never have that in Bradford. I mean, we've all got sewers but who'd have thought to put fucking trains in em?

She coughed at the fumes and smoke that drifted through the tunnels and watched dusty rodents skitter between the tracks. The two girls laughed and tripped up the escalators as they made their way out of the station.

The sunlight broke through the clouds as they walked along Inverness Street, past the market stalls and shops selling fruit and vegetables that they couldn't even name.

Eileen picked up a giant avocado, a papaya, a yam, and laughed at the shapes and colours.

Well, that's a big banana, she said. Only 5p. I'm starving. Let's share one.

When she bit into it and tasted a soft, starchy potato flavour she realised it probably wasn't a banana after all.

Andrea keeled over with laughter as she spat the plantain onto the pavement.

You can take a lass out of Buttershaw, she said. Swear to God I can't take you anywhere.

They walked towards the majestic, columned townhouses that lined Gloucester Crescent, some of them five storeys high. They stared through windows into the opulent living rooms with gold flock wallpapers decorating the interiors. Plush velvet curtains with tie-backs were draped on lofty Georgian frames.

Eileen was aghast. Just look at that, she said. Could you imagine living there? How much does one of them cost?

More than a castle.

I've never seen nowt like it. Can we come back tonight and have another look?

We'll have to pretend we're just walking past, Andrea said. Otherwise they'll think we're on the rob.

The two girls shared a tab and talked about the fit blokes they'd seen already. Eileen stared at a Latino-looking man who walked down the road in an expensive linen suit.

You see, we just don't get fellas who look like that in Yorkshire, she said. They all dress so well down here.

Andrea turned her head and ruffled her hair, just in case he was looking.

So *exotic*. Mick could learn a thing or two!

Don't think he'd get far with his Hai Karate and high-waisters round here . . .

Had it with him, Andrea said. Keeps goin' out with his mates. Down the club. I'm stuck up there on that hill, waiting in every night for him to come back. It's like he doesn't even want to come home. I hate Keighley. It's shit.

What are you going to do? Ave you thought about coming back?

Andrea stopped for a few seconds and rifled through her handbag, pulled her purse out and checked for the keys.

I'll tell him when I get back, she said. Until then, I'm keeping quiet. Only you and Mam know. Another thing, my period's late.

Oh, Eileen replied. Thought you were being careful.

I was, but you know how it is, Andrea sighed. I'm applying to the Association for a flat. Don't think I can cope with having another bairn up there on my own.

As they walked up the steps Andrea pointed to the house over the road.

See that one, over there, with the light on the top floor. And the filthy van out the front.

Yeah.

Well, that Alan Bennett lives there.

Who's he?

Apparently he's a writer. Max said he's from Leeds.

Have you met him, then?

Andrea pushed the keys into the large front door, and lifted the latch which opened into the hallway with polished parquet floors.

No, she said. But I watched him shuffling round in his mac the other day, complaining to himself, the maungy get.

The corridor was lined with original artworks, and framed posters from plays Max had directed. The grandfather clock ticked in the front room, and a small black cat padded its way along the floor, curling its body around their legs and pawing at their skirts. A smooth walnut bowl holding a mound of waxy pomegranates was placed by the telephone.

Andrea lifted Eileen's bag and walked up the wide staircase towards the attic, where two camp beds were laid out. They cracked open a can of lager and peered out of the hatch as vapour trails appeared in the bright blue sky.

Do I get to see the rehearsals?

They might let you in, Andrea said. I'll have to ask.

Who's playing Yousaf? And you?

This bloke called Paul. Scouser. Told me he grew up in care. Was in Borstal for a bit. Then became a singer.

Been in owt on the telly?

Crown Court. I like him. He's not like the others. Been a carry-on though ...

With Paul?

See, he's half-caste. African family. And Yousaf's Pakistani. Some actors got wind and started a protest outside the theatre. Said they should have had the chance to audition. Said a black man shouldn't play a Pakistani. They had banners. Shouted at Paul when he arrived. He had no idea what was going on until he got there. Now he has to leave by the back entrance.

What did he think about it?

Says if you're an actor you should be able to play any part, any colour, any person – man or woman. That's what acting is. Pretending.

Eileen lay back on the bed and pulled her socks off. She stretched out her arms and sighed.

What's it been like, apart from that?

Max writes notes all the time. His writing's so small it's like mouse scribble. Can barely read it. Then he does this thing where he tells each actor a secret about the character, in private. The others don't know. Then when they act it, it all kicks off. And they get angry with each other.

119

Doesn't sound like much fun. Do you have to sit there all day?

Yeah, but then when I listen, I make notes on the script and then they change it. Keep telling them, it's not like that. It didn't happen that way. Don't say it like that. You don't sound like you're from Bradford. Roll the d, so it's a t. Bratfud. They keep getting it wrong. But I get em told anyway.

I'll sneak in tomorrow, with some tinnies, Eileen said. We can watch from the seats.

*

It was a warm, sticky London night, and Andrea was confined at the Court attempting to finish the final scene. Max was furious that she hadn't completed it as she had spent the previous few days getting rat-arsed with Eileen and visiting tourist attractions.

You're not supposed to be getting drunk, he said. Your time here is for writing. Not going out.

He cooked a corn-fed roast chicken with tarragon and served it with mangetout. The girls sat around the dining room table and giggled behind their hands. They whispered as he served up the portions.

Max started eating. Eileen pulled a face. Andrea pushed the chicken around the plate with her fork.

Sorry, not hungry, she said.

You've barely eaten all day, Max said. You can't be more than eight stone.

Seven and a half. Skinny. Even me watch is falling off.

Try and eat, please, it will help you concentrate.

Don't like food much, she said. This chicken tastes rank. Like aniseed balls.

Andrea turned up her nose and placed her knife and fork on the plate.

How about some vegetables? Max asked. Try the mangetout.

She put the pods into her mouth, grimaced, and spat them out onto the plate.

Is this what you call food down here?

Max stood up and pulled her plate away.

If you don't like it I'm sure the cat will.

He turned to Eileen and began to speak in a slow, calm voice that masked the rage rising up his throat.

What about you? Do you think my cooking's below par?

Prefer pie, she said. But, I'll have this bit. Not being ungrateful or owt. It's just, well, we're not used to food like this.

I don't think Andrea's used to any food, is there anything you do eat?

Chips. Not peas, she said. Crisps. Mints. Beef. Not gravy.

Max opened a bottle of wine and poured himself a drink; it swirled around the crystal glass as sediment stuck to the rim.

I'd offer you some of this, but you probably only drink lager.

I'll try it, Eileen said and nudged Andrea. Go on, have a swig. What is it?

Châteauneuf-du-Pape. 1974. A travesty to drink it with chicken, of course.

Don't know what you're on about, Andrea said. Over the top of my head.

He sat down on the sofa, which was draped with velvet throws, crossed his legs and tapped his foot along to a jazz record that played in the background.

So, tell me how things are on the estate at the moment?

Nowt changes there, Eileen said. Same old.

Come on! he shouted. There must be something juicy you can tell me about.

Andrea stretched out on the Persian rug and traced its pattern with her fingertips. Behind her, Eileen slurped the wine from her glass which left a burgundy smile on the edge of her lips.

Well, we could tell him about Julie ... Not bad this, I'll have another ...

Andrea zipped her mouth and glared at Eileen.

Oh, go on, Eileen said. He'll love that one.

Max slapped his thighs and began to speak in slow but excitable manner that barely masked his impish curiosity.

You do realise I have no idea who these people are so it doesn't matter either way. Pray, tell?

Strange things happen on Buttershaw, Andrea said. Well, one of our mates ...

Eileen started laughing, but tried to keep it in, snorting through her nostrils.

Julie, Andrea said. She had this baby. Still at school. Bit of a boiler. Anyway. It were born with no skin.

How awful, Max said. What a shame.

Turns out it had no skin because its Dad were her brother, Steve. What a creep.

Andrea put her head in her hands, sniggering into them, shaking.

Honestly, if you saw him, you'd laugh. Not the bairn. But him. Oh God. He's like Bernard Manning. Don't know how he managed it.

Max took a deep breath.

Not sure how I'm supposed to respond to that, he said.

Might shock you, Max. But for us, it's nowt new. You know. Goes on up there. It's awful, we shouldn't even talk about it. But me and Eileen have been ripping it out of him for years. Then this happened. And t'baby looks just like him. Even wit' skin hanging off!

*

The next day Andrea worked at the Court, and Max suggested scenes to move the play along. Most of them were rejected but it gave her enough material to write her own version. He rambled on about a quote of George Bernard Shaw's: If you're going to tell people the truth, you'd better make them laugh, otherwise they'll kill you. He thought this was particularly apt of Andrea's writing, where northerners deflected hardship through comedy. Black humour was a way of coping with the very worst hand that life had dealt them.

The second act took longer than anticipated and only

twenty-four hours before she was due to return north Max locked her in the upstairs office with a pack of beer until she had finished the draft.

This is what I do to all of my writers, so don't think you're getting special treatment, he shouted through the door. When I come back in an hour this better be done.

Eileen was barred from the theatre until it was completed. They had already picked a fight with an Oxbridge graduate who worked in the office. Andrea shouted that she was a stuck up little cow and threatened to deck her if she looked at her again from the upper stalls.

It was Andrea's nineteenth birthday and she was in a foul mood. Max demanded more detail, and paced up and down the corridor as she frantically completed the final lines of the play. When she walked out of the door and threw the note-pads onto Max's desk she had delivered a second act in which the Girl entered into another fraught relationship and had an unwanted pregnancy.

In capitals, on the last page she wrote the last line of dialogue.

Max was delighted at his new prodigy and raided the petty cash, pushing five quid into her hand.

Now, go and enjoy yourself, he said. Let off some steam. Don't be noisy when you come back.

Thank you, she said.

It was the first time she had ever thanked him for anything. Respect had to be earned. He knew that he must have done something right for any gratitude from Andrea.

*

The girls wandered through the alleyways of Soho that night with an old A–Z map and walked from Oxford Street to Brewer Street, under the arches towards Raymond's Revue Bar. Signs and lights decorated shop fronts advertising hot dogs, books and magazines, non-stop striptease, jazz mags and continental sex films. They stopped outside the Pigalle cinema and stared at the words *Lovecraft*, *Depraved* and *Obsession with Sex* lit up in gold. It was quite unlike anything they had ever experienced.

Red light bulbs glowed in open doorways where carpeted stairs led to dingy flats. Star shaped signs offered Swedish massage for £5 or 'French Polishing' as the stench of urine rose from the side streets. Behind grubby panes and steamed up windows a shadow-play of punters waited in line.

Andrea pointed at the men who shuffled out from behind peepshow stands, as Eileen gawped at the rows of sex shops. When they called Alma from a nearby phone-box they were astonished at the cards shoved into the change slot offering personal services. The worst one, of a twenty-stone woman dressed as a copper, went straight into Andrea's handbag for safe keeping.

That's me Dad's birthday present sorted, she said.

They had been told the Hippodrome was the place to go, but wandered around the pubs first and bought lime cordials in the Pillars of Hercules which they topped up with a half bottle of vodka hidden in their bags. They took the piss out of old lushes who staggered around and put a handful of coins in the jukebox: they drank and shouted and danced to Dexy's Midnight Runners, Madness and UB40.

Leicester Square was the place to visit, that's what their friends in Bradford had told them. They walked past the arch of Chinatown, where pink crispy ducks dripped fat into the vats below, and wondered how they'd ever survive on pints of lager at 45p. The big lights of the square reflected off Chinese restaurants, and the buzz of the crowds excited them. They passed a long line of people waiting to get into a club, some were dressed as Pierrots, others wore tartan pantaloons, the men wore make-up with long, crimped fringes, some had kimonos draped to the floor. Elegant girls smoked through long cigarette holders and blew rings into the air through black painted lips.

Can't tell if it's a man or a woman, Eileen said. What a freak.

Andrea stared at the floor, trying not to laugh.

Wonder how long they'd last on Buttershaw, dressed like that, in polka dot capes.

Never seen owt like it. What a bunch of headbangers.

What was more important to the girls at that moment was finding a proper nightclub where they could go on the pull. In the main square giant hoardings advertised *The Empire Strikes Back* and long lines of people waited to buy tickets under Darth Vader's mask.

The next few hours dissolved into a blur. Too many vodka

and limes. It was their first proper night out since Lorraine was born and Andrea wasn't going to miss the opportunity. Eileen drank two for every one she managed. After midnight they danced to Hot Chocolate under a disco ball at a club called The Whiskey, as cheesy men who came from the suburbs tried to impress them with their moves. They both snogged one with a big moustache. Topless girls danced in cages suspended above the dancefloor and women wiggled around their handbags, attempting to attract attention. Eileen was paralytic by 2am, staggered to the bus stop on Charing Cross Road, and clung to the poles of the Routemaster. After a few minutes of trying to get the key in the wrong door they finally collapsed in a stairwell on Gloucester Crescent, just a few houses down from Max's.

*

The Dunbar family travelled down for the opening of *The Arbor* in the main theatre in June. By the time they arrived at Leeds three fights had broken out and Alma had lost her temper with John Brian, who was still tanked up from the night before.

You know what, Andrea said. I'm made-up that you've all come. It means a lot to me.

She laid the tickets out on the table and re-shuffled them until the inspector arrived. The receipt was £50.

Good job you aren't paying, Pam said. Do we all get to come down every time you do a play?

Rob sent em. Told him, if he didn't send tickets for all of us then I wouldn't come to the opening. So he had to do it. I want a hotel and all, I said. Told him that I'm not coming otherwise. Got tickets a few days later.

Who's Rob?

He reads scripts at the theatre, that sort of thing. But he sorts my contracts out. Meant to be my agent.

Does that mean he takes money off you?

Andrea wiped the table down with a serviette and re-clipped her watch onto her wrist.

10% of everything I earn. Just for sorting the paperwork out. Don't understand it. But that's cheap. There were this woman, Margaret Ramsay, or whatever she's called. Max thought she should be my agent, but she reckoned I could never be a play-wright because I wrote about my own life.

Cheeky cunt, Pam said. What's she mean by that?

Maybe she thinks I'm not up to it . . .

What's her fucking problem? Your play's on at a big theatre, you've been on the box. And in the papers.

Just one of them, Andrea sighed. Most take 20% of everything.

For doing what?

My point, exactly, Andrea muttered. Plus, I've other things to think about. This, for example.

She pulled her blouse up and rubbed on her swollen belly.

Felt it kicking this morning. Been up half the night. Lungs are squashed.

Not like the last one, then?

Bigger. Think it's another girl. I'm certain of it.

The train shot through the flat landscape of Cambridgeshire, as it approached the Home Counties Pam pointed at the houses outside.

Tennis court. Swimming pool. Triple garage, she said. Imagine living there.

Best get filling in your coupons.

Or you can write a hit, buy us one, and we'll all move in! Pam replied.

That sounds about right.

Andrea rolled her eyes.

Tell you what, I'm not arsed about coming to London again.

Alma put down her pen, she had almost filled in her celebrity crossword at the back of *Woman's Weekly*.

What's got into you? she said. Thought you were excited.

Andrea shrugged her shoulders and folded her arms.

S'alright, I suppose. But everyone's just so different down here. Some of em say things like 'I'm skint, can't afford to go out tonight'. And they live in massive houses, wear designer clothes. And I stand there in Pam's hand-me-downs, not a pot to piss in. If they need money, they just go to the box office, borrow from there. Pay it back when they want, no interest. They sit around in rehearsals, arguing, fighting, falling out over what the character thinks or does. They spend all hours at it, then, come the end of the day, they're mates again and go to the pub together. Can't get me head around it ...

Wonder Woman, Alma said.

Eh?

Last clue, then I can post it off.

Pam began to laugh, put a Wrigley's into her mouth and rolled the foil wrapping into a goblet shape.

How would she know that?

Are any of you even listening to me? Andrea said. Like talking to a wall.

No, we're not, Pam replied. Mam's more important things to think about, like winning the crossword and taking me to Torremolinos.

Won't mention it again, Andrea said.

Ooh, sulking now, is she?

Fuck off! Andrea said and kicked Pam under the table.

She peeled open a chocolate bar and started to nibble at the caramel biscuit, chocolate first, until only the wafer remained.

I hope you like the play, Mam. There's loads of new bits. Feel a bit strange about it.

Alma touched Andrea's hand.

You know, we are glad you asked us to come, she said. And at least we'll all be here to look out for you. He'd never admit it, but your father wanted to be a writer once.

Andrea looked over at John Brian, who had just spilled brown sauce onto the new shirt that Alma had bought him for the play. He was covered in sausage roll pastry flakes.

State of him, Alma glared at him from across the aisle.

Andrea whispered from the corner of her mouth.

He's still got all them books in the loft. I remember when

me and Pam went up there one day. Encyclopaedias and maps with bits of paper stuck to them. All his writing. He went mad when he found us rooting about.

That sounds about right. But I think deep down, behind all that front, he's dead happy for you. Never stops talking about you down the pub.

He's a funny way of showing it, Andrea said.

She opened her bag of make-up and applied a layer of mascara which juddered as the train rocked on the tracks.

Honest to God, Alma said. I've never seen him more excited than I did last night.

*

When the curtain rose on the stage's sparse set Andrea stood nervously at the back and chewed her already flaking nails down to stumps. Her fingertips were dry and red-raw, some had started to bleed and were covered in plasters.

She watched the audience with intent from behind the stalls. Listened to what they laughed at, when they fell silent, if they gasped, when they shuffled in their seats.

At the interval she ran backstage to talk to Max, who was busy giving orders to the actors. Andrea pulled on his shirt.

What are they all laughing at? she said. It weren't so fucking funny when it were happening.

You have a gift, he replied. Making an audience laugh is a skill. You're a natural. Enjoy it.

But they're laughing at the wrong bits.

She stomped around the old props balanced against the wall, backstage.

It's like they're laughing *at* me. At Buttershaw. At my family.

It's theatre, not reality. I was concerned some of them wouldn't like it. But did you see their faces?

Max put his arm around her and she recoiled from him, shrugging his touch away from her.

Only trying to reassure you, he said.

Well don't.

She finished her glass with one swig and made her way back down the stairs.

Max gestured to Rob as she slammed the door behind her.

She's like Alfred Wallis, he said. Primitive energy. This play is the dramatic equivalent of Wallis' paintings nailed to the wall of a fisherman's cottage. Her words are the leftover yacht paint.

He paused as the lights began to fade for Act Two.

A world that many try to imitate, but few can convincingly portray . . .

6

Two Nations

In the winter of 1981, the back end of the year, when night began in mid-afternoon and the sun barely reached over the moors, Andrea moved back to Buttershaw.

Before giving birth to her daughter Lisa, Andrea had started work on a new play for the Royal Court. It didn't have a name but was partly based on her and Eileen, Mick, and girls from the estate. In the quieter moments when Lorraine took her afternoon naps she started writing down snippets of conversations and memories of the previous months.

One afternoon she walked into Keighley and picked up a bag of stewing steak for tea, a small sack of potatoes, and a box of Oxo cubes. She spent half an hour in the aisles of WH Smith checking her pools numbers and reading through the magazines. On her way to the bus stop she called in to the market toilets, closed the cubicle and sat down. Toilet paper lined the watery floor and the sanitary bin overflowed. Beyond the door she heard two loud teenage girls talking by the sinks. They were applying make-up and giggling.

It looked just like a sausage! A frozen chipolata! one said.

Did you have a jump? Bet he's a right goer.

Andrea pulled her trousers up and put her ear to the door. She could hear a woman in the cubicle next to her chuckling. And one on the other side. The girls had an audience. Andrea opened her bag, sat down on the toilet lid, pulled out her note-pad and started writing down their conversation.

For the next ten minutes she recorded everything they said, and after they had left she unlocked the door and walked to the sink. Andrea stared at her reflection and grinned. The girls were called Rita and Sue.

*

1981. Back on Buttershaw. More kids than before. Dogs. Dogs. Dogs. Motorbike engines on the grass. Burned mattress on the bonfire. Ford Escort with punctured tyres outside the flat. David said they could get twenty quid for it, for scrap. Joyriders seem to like it. I have to look at the bloody thing every day. Wish somebody would move it.

When we first moved here the grass was taller than me. We played in it. In summer we hid behind the nettles. Mum used to shout us for tea. We tried to keep still, stay quiet, until she lost her rag with us. Pretended we were dead.

The tennis court didn't have a net. But Tony played football on it with his friends, until it got dark. Used their school jumpers for goalposts. They always had mucky faces. It was better then.

Sleeping in my old bed until the flat's ready. Found a box of magazines and books. Read The Stand *before I fell asleep last night and dreamt of Project Blue. There's still a stickman drawing of Dad above the bed. Blu-tack marks on the wall. Always the same here. The smells from the kitchen. The noise outside.*

There's a pile of brown envelopes with my name on the front. From the Inland Revenue. Some in red ink. I'll not bother opening them. They only want to know my business. Only got £600 for the play. Don't know why they need to know any more. I'll put them in the fire, same as usual.

Told Mam that the only brown letters I'll open are giro cheques.

*

A battered MGB made its way through Reevy Road, past the Crescent, and on to Brafferton Arbor. It was a warm day and its windows were down. Andrea watched it cruise past the house three times as classical music blasted from its speakers. Pretending not to notice she kept her head down in the living room as her brothers and sisters took the piss out of the driver.

Look at that twat with the long hair.

Who does he think he is?

Nice car. Will he take us for a drive?

Bet it gets nicked when he comes in.

Max knocked on the door with an assertive da-da-da-da-da-DA DA! Jeanette and Kathy tried to keep their guffaws in, which made it even worse when he walked through the hallway. Andrea barely acknowledged him.

He wore his best silk Paisley shirt for the occasion, a pair of red cords, polished Chelsea boots, and carried a satchel with a typed up copy of Andrea's new play enclosed.

Good afternoon, he said. It's so lovely to see you. Thank you for inviting me here. It's simply *wonderful* to see where you live.

His expensive aftershave filled the room and grabbed at the back of Andrea's throat.

Aye. It's not bad. Sit down. I'll make you a cuppa. Do you have sugar?

She shuffled into the kitchen as Max stared at the framed school photographs on the wall. He ran his hands over the white porcelain dog that sat on the mantelpiece.

Do you have coffee by any chance? he asked.

Mellow Birds. Will that do?

He winced.

Actually, I'll have tea after all. No sugar. Milk. Just a splash.

Max draped his safari jacket over the back of the threadbare three piece suite and listened to the thudding and shouting of the children in the bedrooms above him. Andrea barked at them up the stairs.

Will you fucking shut up! she said. I have a guest. Are you hungry?

She placed a saucer of biscuits in front of him. Bourbons, Rich Tea and Jammie Dodgers.

He took one and dipped it into his tea.

Is that the script, then?

Andrea saw it poking out of his bag and pulled it from the envelope.

Max slammed his hand over the top and took it back, before she had chance to read it.

Now, we need to talk about this, he paused. There are a few things we have to sort out. I think it's about time you got yourself a literary agent. We can't keep doing your accounts.

Isn't Rob looking after that stuff?

She looked out towards the car; a gang of lads had gathered around it and were peering through its back window. The same lads who stole cheese and processed ham from the corner shop and re-sold it to her at half the price.

Andrea bellowed through the front window, which was propped open with a piece of kindling.

Oi. You lot, There's nowt to see round here.

Well, yes, you are right, of course ... Rob is a very busy man. You need a *proper* theatrical agent. To look after business. I feel you could be quite successful and that brings its own responsibilities.

Why should I give all that money away?

She slurped her tea and dribbled a spot onto her new white blouse.

I'm not that bothered, to be honest. I'd rather do it myself.

So be it, but don't say I didn't warn you. Have you thought of a title for it yet?

He sighed and placed the script in front of her. It was the first draft.

I know it's a bit obvious. But I thought *Rita, Sue and Tom Too*. That's what I've been calling it up to now, in any case.

Hmmm. I'm not sure about that. *Tom*. It's not quite right. It should be three letters, though. Something snappy. I've read the script through and that name seemed to jump out. It has to be changed.

They made a list of different names that older men would have on Andrea's notepad.

Ken. Sid. Pete. Bill.

I know, Andrea said. Bob. That's his name. *Rita, Sue and Bob Too*. He's definitely a Bob.

Max nodded and wrote the title down.

Summat's bothering me ...

She paced around the back of the sofa.

It's all good and well writing about my life or people I know, but I need to change some of it. Hide a few details.

Understandable. It's all a matter of disguise.

Andrea sat next to him and blew on her tea.

Used all the same names last time. This new one. Don't want Bob to be too much like Mick. He doesn't deserve it. Besides, it's not really about him. Bob should live in a new-build, have a stuck-up wife. Michelle is in the palace ... a kept woman. So Rita and Sue are his way of letting off steam.

138

Reaching behind the chair she pulled a wooden club from underneath and wrapped it in her hands.

See this? she grinned. This is what Dad used to clobber me with when I were a kid.

He winced as she put it in his hands.

Goodness, he said. How appalling.

We all got a hiding back then, she laughed. Didn't do us much good though.

People say the same about the cane, I was thrashed many a time at boarding school. It was no fun.

The cane? God, that's nothing compared to the club. When Dad's got it in his head you've done summat wrong, then that's it. Me Mam used to go mad. But he still did it. Said it never did him any harm. His old man were even worse . . .

They sat in silence for a few minutes. Andrea perched on the sofa and cleared her throat. Well, I know you've come all this way, she said. But I've stuff to be getting on with. So, have you brought the money?

Max reached into his bag and gave her a roll of notes for her advance.

You'll need to sign this form and date it, put your signature here, he said. Now, this money needs to last. You have to come to London for rehearsals, and you'll need to declare it to the Inland Revenue.

Andrea's sister, Kathy, ran into the living room and interrupted.

Ey, Max. I can do a handstand. Wanna see it? I can act as well. Like the stars on the telly.

Well, that's an admirable quality, he said. I'm sure you are just as talented as your big sister. Do you think you'll become a writer, too?

No. Why would I wanna do that?!

She screamed and ran out of the house into the garden in her bright pink shorts and jellybean shoes.

Max walked out of the front door towards his car. He felt a tug on his trousers as he placed his satchel into the boot. It was Kathy. Again.

I think I'll make a move, he said.

I wanna come with you. Let me sit in the back, she said.

I can't, dreadfully sorry.

Yes you can. Take me with you. Go on. Don't be soft.

Max pushed her away and slammed his door shut as Andrea tutted at him.

I'll be in touch, he said. Kathy, perhaps we'll meet again sometime?

He revved up his car, reversed and drove around the Arbor before heading towards Reevy Road. On his boot, written in the dust, were a few choice words, recently completed by the corner shop gang: *If you think this car is mucky you should meet my wife.*

*

Eileen arrived at Andrea's new flat with a bag of beer, and a Union Jack deely bopper for Lorraine on the morning of the

Royal Wedding. Lisa was old enough to go to her Gran's for the day, and Andrea had been looking forward to her first day without the children since Lisa was born. It had been almost a year of snatched sleep, colic, early mornings and a screaming toddler. On top of that she was already behind on her rent payments.

The flat was on the second floor of Thornby House. On a clear day Andrea could see out across the hills to Tyersal Gate. It backed onto the school fields and caught every draft that blew up the valley. All the same, at least it was hers. She cobbled together bits of furniture from various relatives, and survived on the leccy meter, despite the board's exorbitant rates.

Eileen put the deely bopper on Andrea's head. It dug into her scalp.

Don't think I'll be wearing this today, she said. Ovis! Where are you?

Andrea's nickname for Lorraine was Ovis. Half brown, half white, like Hovis bread. She'd called her that from birth. It was the joke that stuck. Lorraine ran onto her mother's lap and gave her a kiss. Andrea pulled away.

Ugh. Sloppy kisses. Get me a tissue, she wiped her face and Lorraine's. Look. Aunty Eileen's got you a present.

Eileen put the deely bopper on her head.

Do you know, Ovis, you are the most beautiful little girl on Buttershaw. You look like a princess in that.

Lorraine jumped up and down as Eileen hugged her.

141

What do you say? Andrea said.

Um ... thank ... you ... Lorraine whispered.

Andrea fastened up her shoes and they walked her around the block to Alma's before hitting the pub to watch the big day.

When they arrived at the Beacon it was packed out already. There weren't any street parties, not like in the posh parts of Bradford, but a spread had been laid on in the pub and a big telly was connected to the speakers so the regulars could sit and watch it over the course of the afternoon.

John Brian was in his usual place, tanked up and holding court from the end of the bar. Look at that silly cow, he said. More money than sense! They ought to give me some of that cash, I'd spend it right ...

Andrea and Eileen were dressed in white, in tight skirts and sparkling tops. The pub was full, and Jim, who worked behind the bar at the Cap and Bells, was waiting for her when she got there. His face lit up when he saw them.

Now then girls. What a pair of stunners. Finest looking ladies in the pub today. What can I get you?

Half a lager and lime, they chirruped. Starting slow. Going to be a long day.

The Beacon was rowdy and full of the same old faces that had always been there. There was a reliability to the place. It was the estate's hub of gossip, intrigue, corruption, and lies. Everything that happened on Buttershaw passed through its walls. And when John Brian wasn't in there Andrea would sneak in for a crafty pint to pick up lines for her plays. She had even started taking a notebook with her, which she kept hidden in her handbag.

Eileen found them a comfy seat, towards the back of the pub, and together they speculated on what kind of dress Lady Di would wear.

Aw, it's quite nice though, to watch a big do like this. Do you think you'll ever get married? Eileen asked.

I bloody well hope not. Can't say I've ever met anyone who I'd want to marry. All men are the same. They all let you down.

Crowds of people lined the streets of London, and thousands of faces flashed up on the television. Some of them used viewing boxes, in red and white, held against their eyes. When the horse and carriage arrived outside the Cathedral all of the women cheered in the pub.

Ooh, *look* there she is ...

When Lady Di stepped out in her crumpled dress the pub let out a collective groan.

What the hell is she wearing?! Eileen shouted from the back. All that money and she couldn't even afford an iron.

The dress resembled a crushed meringue and her terrified face revealed the emotion of a woman who was making a big mistake.

Well, imagine waking up next to him for the rest of your life, Andrea said. He's an ugly bugger, I'll give him that.

Prince Charles paraded his virginal bride down the aisle and during the vows Janice, the pub's cleaner, burst into tears. This triggered an outbreak of sniffles from the older women in the

Beacon and howls of laughter from Andrea and Eileen who thought the whole thing was completely ridiculous.

Think we're the only ones taking the piss. We keep getting daggers from the corner ...

She'll be refusing to serve us next, Eileen laughed. Don't get on the wrong side of her.

That evening was spent at the Cap and Bells, on Cooper Lane, at the far end of Buttershaw. Like the Beacon, it was built at the same time as the estate, a Magnet sign rattled in the wind over the side door. It had a back room, a dartboard, and a pool table. Andrea pretended to throw darts at Eileen's head as she walked to the bar, the two ended up arm wrestling with Jim after drinking chasers of cheap whiskey.

They staggered back to Andrea's flat and sat up drinking with Jim until the early hours. It was easy to pass the time with him. Andrea and Jim danced in the living room until the first flash of morning light appeared. Eileen laid face down on the sofa, snoring, with her leg balanced on the floor for when the room-spin kicked in.

Jim took Andrea in his arms and squeezed her tight.

You're a cracker, he said. Always was.

She put her face in his chest and rested her head on his shirt.

I can hear your heartbeat, she said. It's sending me to sleep.

He took her into the bedroom, pulled her socks off and they collapsed on top of the sheets. Andrea curled up in a ball with Jim wrapped around her back. It was the first time she had slept for more than three hours in what seemed like years.

In the weeks leading up to the rehearsals of *Rita, Sue and Bob Too*, a letter from Max appeared in the post congratulating her on winning the George Devine Award for Most Promising Playwright with a cheque for £1,000 enclosed. She met up with Pam in the Beacon later that day and gave her a wide beam as she walked through the door.

Bloody hell, Pam said. What's got into you? You're looking chuffed.

Drinks are on me today!

Won the pools have we?

Well, not quite, Andrea replied. But summat almost as good.

The drinkers at the bar raised their glasses to Andrea as she nodded back at them.

Thanks love, they said.

Oh, buying rounds then? Mine's a bottle of champagne and three pickled eggs.

Pam span on the bar stool and tucked her legs underneath.

Been in here since opening, Andrea said. Dad's gone home for a sleep but I'm celebrating.

So, how come you're flush, then?

Won a prize. For the play. They gave me a grand. A whole fucking grand. Can you believe that?

Andrea shook her head in disbelief.

Well, I'll be tapping you up for a loan, our lass.

145

Gonna buy a new suite. Clothes for the girls. Dinner out. Maybe a holiday.

You could take us all to Scarbados!

Seriously, Andrea supped on her drink. Gonna get a tint, proper haircut. Pay off me debts. This is it for me, turned the corner.

Don't be letting this lot know you've got it.

Pam pointed to the drinkers who were splayed around the pub.

You know what they're like. They've got nowt.

No use saying that. They've already written about it in the paper.

Andrea pulled a *Telegraph & Argus* from her bag. Pam squinted at the article and read it out.

Well, I am pleased for you, she said. That's cracking news.

I'm off on holiday for the first time ever. On the pub trip, we're off to Belgium. Can't fucking wait. Big John's driving us in the minibus.

Where you going from?

Catching the ferry from Hull. Then off on a three-day piss-up to Ostend.

Sounds good. Can I come?

Already booked, Andrea said. Off wi Jim. Serve the best chips in Europe. But they put mayonnaise on top. *Euch*. Still, owt's got to be better than a week trapped on the Rochdale Riviera.

146

She gurned and lit her cigarette, blowing smoke rings up towards the sunlight.

Rain, wind and sleet, Pam said. Nowt worse than a week on Hollingworth Lake.

Got to be more to life than the north, she replied.

*

Keep thinking about this play. What can I get away with? Want to write it like people speak, but there's too much swearing. Worried they say fuck too much. That I'll get into trouble.

Max said I can write whatever I want. They can be naked on stage. There's no rules.

Finished a few scenes today:
- *Rita and Sue talk about a man they fancy.*
- *Classroom scene with teacher. Girls get into trouble for talking.*
- *Backseat of a car. With Bob. Having it off.*

They are fifteen. Bob is older.
They are his babysitters.
He is married.

Michelle is Bob's wife. She is frigid. He takes Rita and Sue home one night, after babysitting, and has sex with them in the back of his car, parked on the top of a moor. They take turns having a jump with him. Sue lives on Buttershaw and when she comes home late her Dad threatens her. Thinks she's a lying slag.

Bob's a sparkie. Lives in a posh part of Bradford. One night, when he's out with Rita and Sue he gets spotted by his neighbour who tells Michelle that he's been carrying on with the babysitters. Rita gets pregnant with Bob's child.

The girls think it's funny but Bob doesn't. He knows he could go to prison for messing about with underage girls. Sue dumps him, and Rita is left on her own coping with a baby. Rita and Sue fall out. Michelle gets a divorce, takes all of Bob's money, and he has to sell his car.

In the end Bob is left with nothing.

*

Rehearsals began at the Court in September, and the opening scene, in which Bob has sex with Rita and Sue in his car, was guaranteed to make the audience laugh.

Max gathered the cast and began to speak.

It's essential the comedy works, he said. But this is based on Paul flashing his posterior in the first few seconds. It *must* capture the grim reality of sex. This isn't romantic; it's the cramped fumbling of backseats, uncomfortable positions, steamy windows, biscuit crumbs, cassette tapes and the rain beating down on the roof in a muddy, windswept field . . .

He walked around the room and dropped the script into their laps.

Now, Joanne, Max said. You are playing Rita, and Lesley is Sue. To get over any fear of embarrassment, this week's scene rehearsals will be conducted in the nude.

The cast laughed awkwardly, some turned crimson. Others were pallid with fear.

And that even includes myself, he said. Point being, that the more we do it like this, the less you will notice your nudity in front of an audience. Trust me, I've done this before. It works.

An hour later Max wandered into the rehearsal room wearing nothing except a pair of knee high socks and a grin on his face.

No need for shame, he boomed and brushed his hair over his shoulders.

He moved his meat and two veg into a comfortable position and sat down on the chair.

I'm not doing it, said a voice from behind the curtains.

Max shouted at his assistant, whose face had turned bright purple as he shuffled from behind the set, cupping his testicles behind his hands.

Simon, if you are going to work in theatre, and have a serious career, then you have to get over your reserve. Come on, girls!

Max folded his arms and waited as Joanne and Lesley slowly

peeled off their clothes by the side of the stage. He started writing in his notebook with half an eye open at the naked girls in front of him.

There is a reason for this, and it has absolutely nothing to do with perversion, it's simply to break down the barriers for this scene. Chop chop, I haven't got all day.

This is ridiculous, Joanne whispered to Lesley. Look at their faces.

Paul walked into the room and shook his head.

Well, this is a first, he said.

When Andrea appeared with the new drafts for the script half an hour later she could barely believe what she was seeing.

What the fucking hell is going on here? she shouted from the back. You're not supposed to be in the buff. It's too cold for that sort of thing in Bradford.

It's called *actioning* Andrea, Max replied. You can join us if you want.

Comfortable in my jeans and top, she said. Think I'll sit this one out.

As she walked out of the room Paul created a leg-shaking orgasm move which he amplified for comic effect. When Andrea finally watched the opening scene her head shrank into her neck and she shook uncontrollably as Paul's pink bottom pumped up and down. He passed her test with flying colours.

*

Got the shakes. Could do with another to take the edge off. All a bit much. The people. Everyone asking me things. Interviews. Didn't know what to say. Back hurts. Head hurts. Want to stay in bed for a week.

Show Report said the audience were shocked. A few walked out. The rest were crying, in a good way. Some said it was the funniest play they'd ever seen. That made me feel better. Worth all the bother.

When the music began, that Crazy Bout an Automobile, *Paul (Bob) said look at my hands. How am I going to pull this off? Took some nerve, baring his arse on the stage. I wouldn't. He had a Johnny filled with egg white shoved down the side of the seat.*

Could hear Eileen laughing all the way through. Barking like a seal. Honk. Honk. Honk.

Afterwards she said to him How do you manage to do it twice so close together? Shook my head. Two short planks that one.

There was a full house. Set had broken fences, corrugated iron, mess all over. This isn't like Buttershaw I said. Why have you made it look like a scrapyard?

Max bought me a bottle of champagne. Said getting work out of me was like blood from a stone. That he'd almost given himself a hernia from the stress. But was it worth it? I said. He paused. Taking a bit long to answer that, I said.

Then we drank from his special glasses. They were long, with patterns up the side. Don't break these he said. When I looked down at the glass the light from the bubbles reflected across the table. It was like a mirror ball. After everyone left I walked onto the stage and finished the rest straight from the bottle.

Went to the pub after. Had a fag with Tracey. Told her she played a good Michelle. Have you met Oscar she said. Come over here and sit down. He shook my hand and said Have you ever thought about making a film. Your writing reminds me of some of the things I have worked on. Saturday Night and Sunday Morning. Billy Liar. Taste of Honey. *Not that fussed I said. Don't like films much. But he kept going on until I gave him my address. I'll write to you he said. And I kept on drinking into the night.*

*

Lisa ran across the living room carpet as Andrea lay on the sofa, covered by a woollen blanket. The noise of a jack-in-a-box repeated in the hallway as Lorraine re-wound its spring. The girls crawled over their mother as she lay silent with her eyes closed. Balls of paper were crushed beneath her. The debris of the previous night's writing.

The door rattled as John Brian let himself in. He carried two bags of shopping and walked straight into the kitchen. He pulled a can from the bag.

What's up with you then?

Nowt. Andrea said. Just not in the mood for talking.

He sat down in the wobbling armchair, opened the can, took three gulps and let out a sigh.

Do I get a hello?

The girls ran to him and one sat on each knee. His legs were thin and the girls shuffled about, placing a cushion between his legs until they were comfortable. John Brian reached into his pockets.

Grandad's bought you some sweets. Two bags of goodies.

Lisa opened up the white paper bag and pulled out a cola sour. He turned to Andrea.

Are you ill or hungover? Here, he said. Have some of this. That'll sort you out.

He shook the beer can at her.

Andrea started stirring.

Don't need more of that. Already feel like I've been kicked.

He stood up, brushed the sugar off his trousers, and sat down beside her on the sofa.

Shall I take the bairns to Pam's?

Euch, she said. I can smell you from here.

No need to be like that.

Pam's enough on, Andrea mumbled. They're alright wi me.

The cuckoo clock struck one and Lisa pointed at it as the doors flipped open.

Bird, she said. Fly.

Don't think I want to write again, Andrea said. Papers have been at me.

Thought you liked it. You've had some brass. No point giving up now.

They've stopped me fucking giro, haven't they. Read the paper, with the announcement. About the prize. Someone grassed me up. Now I've nowt coming in. Dole office have stopped my cheques. Wish I'd never bothered in the first place.

He grimaced and cracked his knuckles together. Click. Click.

Wish you wouldn't do that, she said. And I wish you'd wear your teeth.

Here, have this. Was me Dad's, he said. And Grandad's. It's yours.

He lifted a gold chain from around his neck and dropped it into her hand.

Andrea held it up as it twinkled against the light.

Remember him wearing it. Are you sure?

Take it, he said. Pawn it if you have to. Buy it back later. It's all I've got.

Andrea gave him a soft punch in his left arm.

I'll look after it, promise.

That Jim looking after you alright?

Yeah. Bought me a charm bracelet for Christmas.

Your proper boyfriend now, is he?

Maybe. Suppose so ...

Andrea paused and cocked her head to one side.

What are you two doing in my room? she yelled. I can hear paper being torn in there.

Nothing! The girls shouted.

Nobody's ever bought me owt like that before. Gave it me in a heart-shaped box with velvet inside. I'll show you it.

Andrea walked into her room and began to shout.

Lorraine! What the fucking hell have you done? That's my writing. How did you get that down from there?!

Paper, Lorraine said. To draw.

That's my script. Telling me you climbed on that wardrobe to get it?

Sorry, she said. Did colouring.

Andrea picked up the bracelet and showed it to John Brian, who was already onto his second can.

Here, she said. A wishing well with a handle and jug inside. A Charlie Chaplin car, that's for our rides out on Sunday afternoons. Yorkshire's White Rose, that's what he calls me when I'm drunk.

A rose? he sniggered.

Ballet pumps with a bow, that's because I fall flat on my arse most of the time. Each letter of my name spelled out on keys to remind me, in case I forget ... basket of pearls, for the money that's coming my way. A thimble, for when I worked at the mill. An old boot with a cat and mouse hidden inside, think that's him and me running away from each other. This one. Second favourite. A little teapot, because I'm always having a brew. Twenty-one for the age I was when we first met. But, out of all them, I like this. Palm trees on a tropical island. One day we'll go sit on a beach abroad.

Must be serious, he said. All that effort.

I don't do *serious*. All fellas are alike, when it comes down to it. I mean, not many do the right thing.

Not for lack of trying. I've always worked hard, he said.

You haven't worked for twenty years, what are you on about?

I work.

Do you bollocks work, she said. Work down the pub, more like.

*

Third time lucky, 1984. All of us on Barden Avenue. No money coming in. I finally have a boy, Andrew. At least he sleeps, but I don't. Haven't seen Jim this week. I'm used to getting my own way.

He tries to tell me what I should think and say.

Older men are like that.

Think you don't have an opinion of your own.

Partly my own doing, the fights. Can't help myself. So this is how it is. He lives at his, I live at mine. He takes Andrew out when I need a break. Sometimes takes the girls.

Should be writing, but can't. Need to lock myself away. Lock the kids away, more like. Can't concentrate. Even writing this is hard. Feels like I've run out of words. Supposed to be thinking about this script.

Oscar wrote last week. He lives near Brighton, in a big house by the beach. Sent me a picture of it. The light is shining behind and he has wisteria growing up the windows. Told me his wife makes pots that look like the sea. They have waves on them. Giant vases and jugs. She has an art studio next to the house and he has a library full of books on theatre and film that I can use any time. Says I can write in there and finish the script. He'll help me with the screenplay. It's going to be made into a film based on The Arbor *and* Rita, Sue and Bob Too. *My life on a cinema screen.*

He's booked tickets for the National Express. Only eight hours from Bradford. Andrew can come with me. There's a big room at Oscar's for me to sleep in with white cotton sheets and I can look at the sea every day. Doughnuts and candyfloss stalls on the promenade. We can throw skimmers and paddle in the water.

It's a place where the sun always shines.

*

When Andrea returned from Oscar's she turned her back on writing until the money finally ran out. Max, who had been her point of contact at the Court, was too busy to work with her, and Rob had left the theatre.

His replies became slower, and her suggestions for new ideas were knocked back. By the time 1985 came around she had stopped writing altogether. Carole, Max's ex-wife, offered to direct *Shirley* in the Theatre Upstairs, as part of the Short Sharp Shock season.

Andrea had watched Carole onstage at the Court in Caryl Churchill's *Top Girls*, which was first performed in 1982, just before *Rita, Sue and Bob Too*. Andrea watched all of Caryl's plays at the Court. Her notes and ideas were sent to Carole's house near Clapham, in south London. She was desperate for money and over the course of a few months Carole journeyed backwards and forwards to Bradford to work on the script. Andrea didn't like workshop situations and it was difficult to get her to write. It was an even bigger struggle for Carole.

Throughout the rehearsals Andrea stayed at Carole's house

and brought Andrew with her. Each night Carole sat her at her kitchen table with a pack of beer and forced her to create characters and scenes. Some nights she only managed to write one line. On others she'd write three pages of perfectly formed dialogue. It was always a battle. For Andrea, everything was black and white. She hated most of Carole's ideas.

One evening they argued over a key scene which Andrea wanted to include, which was based on her friend Maureen.

You see, Carole, Andrea laughed. I think it would make a good scene. I want her to be a character, one of Shirley's Mam's mates.

It's a dreadful idea, too close. People won't take it seriously. It's tabloid.

What do you mean by that? It fucking well happened. It's not made up you know.

How many drinks have you had today? Carole asked.

Not enough, she smirked.

We've been rehearsing all day and you've only a couple of days left until it needs to be handed in, Carole tapped her fingernails on the kitchen side.

Yeah. That's why I want to do this scene with Maureen in it.

Do you think it will add anything to the play? Seriously?

I've done this bit. Wrote about her blackouts ...

Andrea's words began to slur.

I'll read some out if you don't believe me.

Go ahead, Carole replied.

Carole sat down at the kitchen table amongst the detritus

of paper, fag ends, biros and crisp packets. Andrea cleared her throat, *MAUREEN: I've got these scars in my head. I know it were him who did it. He crept up on me . . .*

Stop! Really, Andrea. You're going off the point here. This needs to be about Shirley and her mother. You already have a friend and three additional male characters. This won't add anything to the play. You need to focus.

Well why don't you just fucking write it yourself if that's what you want?

Andrea stood up and wobbled behind the chair.

Carole patted her hand on the table and sighed.

We need to get through this. I'm trying to help. This isn't easy for any of us.

Andrea's tiny frame swayed to one side. She belched and walked towards the fridge.

Is that my vodka you've been drinking? You've had half a bottle. I only bought it last week. Christ, you really need to slow down.

Don't fucking tell me . . .

Andrea splashed fresh orange into her glass and necked it in one go. Carole pulled out a packet of mince from the fridge.

Have you eaten today? Let's have dinner and then we can try to finish the script. How does that sound?

Huh. Well, we can *try* to do that, Andrea replied. But I'm not happy about what happened at rehearsal. When I say slamming school, I fucking mean it . . .

Thought we'd agreed to disagree on that one?

Andrea pulled a face behind Carole's back.

It's an actual word that we say in Bradford, she said. So it's going in.

Carole took a deep breath and started chopping onions frantically as the steam from a pan of boiling water began to fog the kitchen over.

And another thing . . .

Yes?

How did you manage being married to Max for all them years?

That's a long story, Carole replied.

Andrea rocked backwards and forwards and reached towards the chair.

Sorry, she said. For drinking your vodka.

If it helps you finish the writing then so be it.

I like getting shit-faced. It helps. I can forget about everything. Stops the fire coming off me head.

It's not unusual, writers getting drunk. Writing's not easy.

Carole crushed the garlic cloves and began to fry them in the pan.

Huh. Nowt's easy. Life's not easy. It's just when I'm drinking I can switch the noise off. Tune out for a bit.

Andrea picked up a piece of paper, she held it to her face and started to read the lines.

Can you pass me the basil, on the windowsill?

Basil? What the fuck's that?

It's a herb.

Carole squeezed a leaf between her fingers.

Like a smoke? Bit of wacky baccy?

No, you eat it. It goes in Italian food, like spaghetti. I'm making you some.

Carole pushed it under Andrea's nose.

But it's a plant, she winced. I'm not eating that. *It stinks*.

You have to eat something, Carole said.

Already had some toast.

Andrea stood up, her legs wobbled as she walked towards her room and she knocked into a table in the corridor. She proceeded to projectile vomit up the stairs and collapsed face down on the bed, fully-clothed.

I'm not coming back here, she shouted from the other room. I'll find somewhere else to stay next time.

*

The rehearsals for *Shirley* took place in the Theatre Upstairs, and Andrea made notes as each actor spoke. Ed, the singer from Tenpole Tudor, played Simon.

Andrea was subdued and the staff barely spoke to her through the day. Ed sat next to her and made her laugh.

The north is a fine place! he shouted. And I've been made an honorary member of Park Hill Flats in Sheffield.

Never been to Sheffield, she replied. Too far.

I was in a band, so we were up there touring, I've spent plenty of time up there. The people are genuine. Unlike in here!

Andrea groaned.

Too polite by half, he said. Problem is, you never know what they are thinking. If they're telling the truth. They could hate you and you wouldn't know it. That's no way to live.

He crossed his giant spindly legs, tapped the mud off his army boots and started rolling a cigarette.

Why are you acting, then? she said.

Bit of cash, do it now again. Prefer playing rock and roll to be frank, but – a bit of this is bread and butter, if you know what I mean?

Saw you on *Top of the Pops* once.

Fame! We all deserve our fifteen minutes. Now, he said. Tell me where you are staying?

Hers.

She nodded at Carole.

I've recently moved out of the squat, and have a penthouse of my own. Would you like to sleep on my sofa instead? he asked. It's a bit flea-bitten. But at least you can get away from this lot.

He pointed at the staff who were crouched around a copy of the *Guardian*.

That'd be nice, she said. I'd like that.

The only tax is that you have to wash up. In return, I can offer you a tour around the delectable sights of Finsbury Park. This morning, before you arrived, I turned up with a newspaper under my arm. Picked it up on the bus. Did half the crossword on my way here. Anyhow, walked in the door, and at least three people looked at me with disgust for reading the *Times*. Apparently it's not the done thing.

He rolled his eyes.

You see, they love to put on working-class writers in here, but it has to be in the theatre, where it's safe.

I read the *Sun*, Andrea said. And *Weekly World News*.

You keep it that way, he replied. Just don't let them know what you're up to. Half have never left north London, Bradford's like another country to them.

Think they've had enough of me in here.

What makes you think that? he said.

Keep complaining about all the tickets I ask for. Don't like coming down on my own. Nobody to talk to, so I need people with me. It's better that way.

Ed re-lit his roll-up and fastened the torn patch on his jeans with a safety pin.

I've got beer in my bag, he said. And a joint. Shall we go sit outside? It's a fine day.

They walked through the traffic on Sloane Square and sat on a bench overlooking the theatre. Ed opened the top on a can of beer and handed it to her.

Have you seen the *Road* script yet? he asked.

No, been too busy.

Started the rehearsals yesterday, it's very good you know. They think it might be transferred downstairs.

Andrea scrunched up her face.

I'm stuck up there, she said. On the scrapheap.

Don't think of it like that, I mean, Jim's just Max's favourite now. That's how it goes.

She slurped on her can and sighed.

Still have to finish this thing for Oscar, she said. I shouldn't be too fussed about it.

What happened with Max?

Nothing. It's just, he tried to ring, and I couldn't answer. Lost touch with each other. I didn't do what I said I would on time. Once he rang up and the kids had set the bedroom on fire . . .

Ed threw his head back and laughed.

That's a great excuse, I must use that one, he said.

It's hard, the kids don't behave. Once Lorraine stuck her fingers in an electric socket. Then she ripped up the script I'd written and Max had typed up. Had to stick it back together with tape.

How punk! he said.

Still want to write, but don't have the time or money. Just do it when I've a spare week or two. It's hard enough trying to stay alive, never mind thinking about this damn place.

7

Shooting the Messenger

It was a sleepy afternoon in the Fox & Hounds, a small Victorian pub just around the corner from the Royal Court on Passmore Street, a few hundred yards from Sloane Square. The walls were decorated with amaranth paint and framed prints of hunters and hounds were hung on the walls. Landed gentry chased wily foxes on muscular white horses that frothed at the mouth. Their red jackets, riding boots, camel breeches and whips punctuated each alcove of the pub as stuffed vixens crouched on the bookcases beside them. Their once-luxurious coats had disintegrated and Andrea stared at the fox's amber eyes as she sank swift halves in the afternoon light.

The theatre's cast gathered in its smoky rooms in between rehearsals. Polished brass decorated the bar and its tables were mottled and copper-topped, heavyweight ashtrays overflowed on each corner. It was the perfect location to discuss the film production of *Rita, Sue and Bob Too!*, which had just received funding from British Screen and Channel 4.

Patsy was a casting director, and already had an idea about Rita and Sue, the kind of characters they were. There was a familiarity already. She had an easy way about her, and any reserve that Andrea initially had was quickly dispelled after four pints of lager and an afternoon of smoking tabs in the Fox.

As the nicotine filtered into the fug that clung to the bar ceiling Patsy began to tell Andrea about her life growing up in east London.

Wasn't easy growing up back then, she said. I was one of six; we lived in a small terraced house. Had to top and tail in single beds. I'm really impressed by what you've written. Considering this is your first attempt. It's still quite raw, but I can see how it will work.

She began to read some of the scenes on her lap.

Never knew it were like that down here, Andrea said. Allus thought there were money in London.

No, it's not like that at all.

The barmaid wiped down the sticky patches on the table in front of them.

I grew up on next to nothing. My parents are Irish, we were treated like shit in London. It was impossible to rent anywhere, there used to be signs up in the windows saying No Dogs, No Blacks, No Irish.

If you come to Buttershaw you'll see what it's like. Families of ten stuck in a two bed flat. Kids running around every-where. No jobs. At least you have that down here. At least there's some hope.

Andrea removed her jacket as Patsy underlined some of the dialogue of the script.

Maybe so, Patsy said. But for my Dad, well, he couldn't even read or write. I had to read for him when I was a kid. Sort out the bills, write letters to the bank. We really struggled. But that was then ...

Andrea pointed to the rings on Patsy's fingers.

You've done alright for yerself now though. Not bad all things considered.

Not without a fight, Patsy laughed and pulled out a page of the script. Now, this section here, have you thought about a scene where they all meet each other and argue. Something on the estate, with Bob and the girls, and Michelle. A confrontation.

Yeah, I've tried to write it already but I can't quite get it right yet ... I know you keep saying it's going to be a film. The thing is, I haven't had any money. And I'm skint. Had to lend off Jim to come here today. If it's going to happen then you have to sort me out.

I know, Patsy replied. You see, the way the industry works Andrea, you get your money on the first day of filming; that's the same for everybody who's involved. The rest comes when it opens in the cinema.

But why should I have to wait? Andrea shrugged. It's taken

so long. Nearly two years. I've three kids to feed. Oscar said I'd get seven grand.

We can't just bend the rules for you. That's the way it is. The actors have it the same, so do the directors. None of us get paid until the filming begins. It's hand-to-mouth. Channel 4 are helping fund it, I might ask if there's any leeway.

Andrea tutted and finished her pint.

Hand-to-mouth? People in London have no idea what that means. You try living on a giro cheque, she laughed. I'm behind on everything, rent, clubman; I even owe my Mam money. Can't expect Jim to support me ...

It must be tough on you, she paused. And you've done all the hard work already. But it will be worth it, in the end. Patsy pulled out a letter from the producer. Sandy thinks the film will be a massive hit. If that happens, well ... you'll be a very rich lady.

As the barmaid gathered the empty glasses from the table Andrea noticed a man walking through the doorway wearing a flat cap. He wore a quilted jacket and had curly hair. He nodded at Patsy. Oh, here's Alan, I'm sure you'll get on like a house on fire.

He gestured at her and pointed to the bar.

Two for us. Yes, we'll have a chaser with that, too.

Andrea moved her coat out of the way and made a space beside her. Patsy began to speak.

Alan made a film in the late 70s, called *Scum*, she said. It was banned by the BBC for being too close to real life. There was a scene in a gymnasium, where two gangs – one black, one white – kicked the living daylights out of each other. He pitched one against the other and stirred it up before he switched the camera on. You know, I'm convinced he's the right person to make your film.

Hello Andrea.

Alan leaned over the table and shook her hand. He had a firm grip, and big hairy palms.

It's good to meet you, at last. Sorry I'm late.

Oh, Alan. Only two hours late this time. It's a vast improvement ... we call this 'Alan-time'. You run on your own clock, don't you?

You might have guessed I'm from Liverpool, he said. Haven't been to Bradford since, ooh, must be 1971.

He squinted and removed his flat cap.

Made a film there called *Horace*. I know Halifax quite well, all those blackened chimneys, the steep valley, the smog from the mills. Anyhow, he continued. I spent many a day shooting on the tops. We filmed it on Whitsun, it was fucking freezing. Everything was shut. Cost us next to nothing to make. I got arrested after getting pissed and tripping over the grill in the hotel. Got in all sorts of bother ...

That's not far from us, Andrea said. The estate's closer to Halifax than Bradford. It's up on the hill, the highest point. That's why the Beacon is called that. If you come up I'll take you for a pint.

Oh, I won't be going back to Halifax, that's for sure. The police don't like me there ...

He leaned towards Andrea and pushed his hair back. See this, he pointed to a scar on his face.

That's a bit deep. What happened?

Andrea touched the zigzag shape that ran along his hairline.

The coppers threw me down the stairs. I went in to the station and complained; they'd been harassing me all week. Kept following me around in the car. I was filming. Had a few run-ins with them ...

They actually did that to your head? Patsy said.

Yeah, they did. It was at night, I went in to talk to them about the way they'd treated me. Told them a thing or two. The main guy behind the desk, some fat-neck with a radish face, well, he got redder and redder. I shouted, he came round the desk, and took hold of me. He pushed me down the stairs. Christ! I had to have ten stitches that night.

Alan laughed and finished his whiskey.

It's not the first time I've heard that. Dibble are right shits in Halifax, Andrea replied. Think you'd hit it off with my Dad.

*

In the early summer months of 1986 Alan and Patsy hired a space for auditions in the back room of an Oldham theatre. They invited a northern actor, George, to audition for the part of Bob. Michelle, who was from Rochdale, was being considered for Sue's role, and a series of other girls auditioned for the part of Rita.

Throughout the day they tried out key scenes from Andrea's script and chopped and changed the parts between actors. The room had tall windows and long velvet curtains. They sat on a pair of chairs in the centre of the parquet flooring and made notes.

One of the taller actresses, Siobhan, was twenty years old, and had only acted in amateur dramatics around the Oldham area. She'd heard about the part through her boyfriend. She was shy, but thought it was worth having a go.

What will you do if you don't get this part? Patsy asked.

I'll probably sign up for a job at Kendal's selling spirographs and cuddly toys in the children's department again, she replied. School didn't want me to be an actress. They said it was stupid for girls like me to think about jobs like that.

The casting call had asked for the girls to dress rough; they were looking for performances that were graphic and modern. Most of the actresses, even though they were only young, looked over forty. Siobhan wore a punk outfit and backcombed her hair. She certainly didn't look fifteen, which was the age for Rita.

She looks too old, Alan said. Not sure if she's right.

Give me a minute, I'll be back, Siobhan replied and ran into the toilets. She scrubbed her make-up off with Izal paper, flattened her hair, removed her jewellery and walked back into the room with a teenage stride that convinced Alan she was almost perfect.

I can already see the camera tracking her, he said.

As the day progressed the numbers dwindled and Siobhan

read the parts of Rita and Sue with Michelle until Alan and Patsy decided who should play who.

What are we going to do about George? Patsy said. I've known him for years, he used to be a woodcutter, you know. I'm sure he'll be perfect.

George gestured at her as he walked into the room. He wore a naff pair of grey silver trousers and loafers for his costume with a shirt buttoned down to reveal his chest. Alan was less enamoured when he stumbled on his lines, missed the jokes and screwed up the timing,

I can play this part with my eyes closed, George said. Just having an off-day, that's all.

I've come across a few like you over the years, Alan replied. You have the patter, but it's not enough. We'll have to keep looking. There's somebody better out there.

Following the audition George tracked Alan's number down and called him in his hotel, much to his own embarrassment.

I'm sorry Alan, he said. About today. I was crap. I wouldn't hire me, either. But you have to understand that there's something about Bob that connects with me. I wouldn't have rung you otherwise.

Oh right, Alan said. On your knees?

In some way, yes. I'm the only person who can do this role justice. Please, just give me another chance.

After an hour of pleading Alan relented and invited him back to the next day's audition. When he arrived George displayed a mighty performance of a male chauvinist pig. His lines were flawless, as was his Bradford accent, which he had been perfecting until the early hours of the morning. The day after that, the part was his.

When the rehearsals for the film finally began, a few months later, George, Michelle and Siobhan met at a school in Bradford, and for two weeks they rehearsed every scene like a play. Alan had a background in theatre and insisted this method was the best way of removing any embarrassment from the filming.

Yes, he said. There are sex scenes, but the film won't be sexy. The movement and delivery of the lines *have* to be pitch-perfect.

The three actors took turns to lay on a camp-bed and practised the various scenes. George gave Michelle's breast a comedy squeeze in the first scene, they both laughed. After ten squeezes it became just another movement they had to do. It had no significance.

At 4pm every day Alan fed Siobhan and Michelle slices of Battenberg and made the cast a cup of tea. He looked after them. But Andrea was nowhere to be seen. She was barred from rehearsals.

When the cast asked if she was coming to watch he laughed.

No way, she's not coming in here, he said. I don't want her hanging around saying 'no'. It's obvious that we'll fall out at some point; it's not a question of if, more a question of when. It's my version of *Rita, Sue and Bob Too!*, not hers. This has to be done my way.

*

173

When Alan arrived in Bradford he spent his evenings drinking in the pubs around Buttershaw and went on the piss with John Brian. He called in to see Andrea and took her out to the Beacon, where he held court and caused chaos. His scouse accent became stronger and a crowd began to follow him as he wandered like the Pied Piper through the streets down to Cross Lane Liberal Club, one of Andrea's favourite haunts.

He sat with Andrea, eating a pickled onion and a packet of scratchings, as a local turn took to the stage and told a variety of mother-in-law jokes over the microphone.

See him, he said. He's funny. I mean, you'd never hear anything like that in London.

Patsy covered her mouth.

Eh, Pats. Did you hear that?

Yes, she replied. I heard it. Don't you worry about that.

Tell you what though, I do have a question. What's the worst music you've ever heard?

Andrea paused.

How about Shakin' Stevens, he's pretty bad, she said.

Not as bad as Renee and Renato, Patsy replied. Or *Je Suis Un Rockstar*.

Don't really listen to much music, used to like Slade and David Essex at school ... Dad were into Elvis, all that fifties stuff.

I'm not asking what you did like, Alan said. Or what was *good*. Don't want anything that's tasteful. It's all about scraping the bottom of the barrel. See, it's for the soundtrack. That scene we're doing at Lilycroft working men's, the Bierkeller night, Bob, Rita and Sue on the dancefloor. With Fat fucking Mavis . . .

What's the name of that Bradford band, awful? Patsy said. Smokie! How about them?

Nah, Alan replied. Too serious. I need a band far worse than Smokie.

Well there is another, said Andrea. Used to play in the clubs around here. Allus on at kids' parties.

Oh no, not them.

Yes. Them. Black Lace, why hadn't I thought of that before? Music for brain donors, he said. Absolutely perfect.

A wide grin appeared across Alan's face.

Andrea shook her head.

Are you serious? *Agadoo* and the fucking *Birdie Song*? Not that record . . .

Alan clicked his fingers and started to concentrate.

The other, *meh meh meh* – the Conga. That's what we need, a song just like that. Andrea, he continued. You are a genius.

Around the bar a gang of young men handed out pints of bitter. Some were dressed in stonewashed jeans, Fred Perry shirts and red braces. Others wore Sergio Tacchini tracksuit tops and had wedged haircuts.

You know, when we shot *Made in Britain*, I used to go out drinking with Tim. He played a skinhead, Trevor . . .

Like the ones in here, stood at the back?

Yeah, but his character was worse. Aggressive, proper psycho. Swastika on his forehead. Borstal lad.

There's a few of them around here, she replied. Call themselves the Ointment.

Why's that? he said.

Summat to do wi Millwall, like the Treatment. A pisstake I think. They used to dress up all in white before a game. With bowler hats and eyelashes drawn on one eye. There's one called Plank, who walks around with a bit of wood in his trousers so he can batter people.

Unpleasant, I can imagine. But those sort of people, they interest me, he said. Violence *interests* me.

You wouldn't think that if it were happening to you, she said. Trust me, it's no fun waking up next to a fella who's kicked your head in the night before.

I like your uncomfortable truths, Alan said. That's why I'm making this film.

He stood up and walked over to the slot machine, put in a few coins and started playing on the buttons, which whirred and buzzed and beeped as the coins started to clatter down through the machine.

He tells his actors a line before they start filming, Patsy said. You'll see him do it when we begin. I've heard it many times. He always says *let the pig out, let's have a good look at him, then let's kill him!*

What does he mean by that? Andrea said.

The pig's everything that's wrong with Britain. It's Maggie, society, inequality, disaffected youth. The usual. He's a socialist, isn't he?

I don't even know what that's supposed to mean.

Don't think they do, half of the time, Patsy said.

*

Eileen, Jim and Pam all spent time with Alan and Patsy in the pub over the next few weeks. Alan caught taxis back to his hotel each night and made extensive notes on the accent and location into the early hours before falling asleep.

For George, Andrea had all the information he needed to do the part justice. He spent three nights with her in the Beacon attempting to get a sense of how he should play the part.

You're a bit of an arsehole, really. Aren't you? she said.

Think you're just testing me.

How can a middle-class person play Bob?

I'm not fucking middle-class. Well, maybe compared to you I am, he replied.

They played the pub quiz together and George won eight pints which were distributed around the bar, he was popular after that. Bob's character was a lot rougher than George's; it was essential he got every detail right.

Andrea grilled him about minor details in his character. If he was going to play a man based on her ex, then he had to have the right credentials. He was much better looking than any of her boyfriends, but had bright blue eyes and a smooth-talking manner, and that appealed to her.

I can see why Patsy cast you, she said. What does Bob drink?

Lager, he said.

Wrong. It's bitter. Mild. Does he like sport?

Football, Bradford City. And definitely cricket.

Not sure about that, she said. He's a rugby league man.

Who's his favourite singer?

Luther Vandross.

Correct. Where does he buy his underpants?

Marks and Spencer.

M&S?! As if. It's the fucking market you silly cunt, knock-off Calvin Kleins. And his wife would buy them.

He immediately bowed to her wisdom.

Silly me, he said. Should've known that one.

*

Filming started this week. It's costing almost a million to make. Doesn't feel right, blowing all that money on my play. I mean, that's really what it is, when it comes down to it. When I think about all that money I feel sick. Paddy in the pub thinks I'm in the money now. Keep telling him, I don't get that money you know, it's to make the film. But try telling him that. He keeps asking me to buy him a drink. The whole of Buttershaw wants me to buy their drinks. They treat me different now, since the film crew arrived and since it all appeared in the paper. Dad said I'll do a Viv Nicholson and blow it all on fur coats and cruises. He reckons I'll end up back on the Arbor no matter what happens.

Bumped into Maureen yesterday, outside the shop. She was steaming. Alan was there. I told him about her. So now he wants her in the film. He said she's got the right type of face. She won't speak, it's a cameo, as Rita's mum. He thinks she'd look good in rollers and a dressing gown.

Then he drove me up to Baildon, to watch them film the opening scene, in the car, with George.

Alan kept asking George to re-do the bit where he finishes with Rita and Sue and walks off to the field to have a piss. It went on for ages. Took about ten goes to get it right. Siobhan and Michelle were wrapped in blankets, it was freezing up there. Alan told George to talk to his parsnip, as if it were a person. Congratulate him, he said. He's done a great job tonight.

George walked to the dry stone wall, unzipped his fly and stared across the city. He said Yes my son. You bobby dazzler.

Over the car was a tower, a crane sort of thing. A cameraman was on the top, buckled in. It moved as the car drove up the hill. After a few takes the electrics stopped, and he couldn't get back down. He was stuck up there, in the wind, and it was dark. It was alright for the first few hours, but after that we had to send up a flask on a rope. By ten he shouted that he needed a shit. Me and Alan creased up, but he wasn't joking. He had to have one. But he was stuck. So Alan sent a bucket up with a toilet roll inside. He shat in the bucket and sent it back down.

Never laughed so much in my life.

*

When the film crew arrived on Buttershaw half of the estate turned out to watch the filming. Family, friends, and neighbours loitered around the cameras and commented on the proceedings. Shoeless children ran around the streets, their faces smeared with the remnants of snotty noses and chocolate. The crew brought them sweets every day; many had never witnessed such poverty.

Extras were recruited from the estate, and school scenes were filmed in the classroom and grounds at Buttershaw Upper School, using teenagers who were at a loose end in the summer months.

In between scenes, Andrea drank with Michelle and Siobhan in the Beacon and shared cigarettes with them on the front steps of the pub. Eileen joined them one day and sat with Andrea. Michelle and Siobhan were in costume.

Well, this a bit weird, Eileen said, as she supped on a half in the back bar.

Yeah. It's me and you, and me and you, Andrea laughed. Think you two are better looking though.

I don't know about that. But there's no way we can keep up with you two. We've got lines to learn, Siobhan replied. I've already had three.

Can tell you aren't from Buttershaw . . .

Eileen rustled around in the bottom of her handbag searching for coins.

Have you got any money? I know it's my round but I've only two quid.

Andrea leaned over Eileen's knees and dug deep into her jeans pocket. They were tight and bleached, almost white.

There's a fiver in here somewhere, she said. I must be getting fat. Can't get my hand down there. I don't mind buying for you, you're my friend. But it's getting fucking ridiculous in this place. Even the doctor asked if I want to go private.

Siobhan and Michelle talked about the scenes they had shot the week before, up in Haworth.

A while since we've been up there, eh? Me and Andrea lived up there for a bit. Haven't been back in years. Was it chucking it down?

It rained every bloody day when we lived at Hermit Hole, I mean, it's bad enough up here but that place was the pits, she said. I'm glad I came back.

Andrea's voice was quiet. It was sometimes hard to hear her words, they were barely audible. Even Eileen had to lean in to hear her speak.

We did that scene at the Brontë Parsonage, on the cobbles, Michelle said. We had to keep re-taking the fight, slapping each others' faces. The girls actually battered me. No joke. We really had a scrap, she paused. Had to keep having make-up re-applied. My cheeks were stinging by the end. I packed a good punch though.

Some of the scenes weren't even written by me anyway, Andrea said. Turns out Alan got another writer in. I didn't know anything about it until last night. When I saw the script.

Cheeky cunt, Eileen said. What did he do that for?

181

Haven't even asked him yet. So angry. And upset, actually, more than anything. Andrea took a deep breath. I'm hurt, but then I rang Rob and he said that's what happens in films. They get re-written and it's nowt to do with me after I've handed it in. Even though my name's on it.

He made *Christine* last, didn't he, Siobhan said. About that smackhead. He said he's doing the same type of shots with me and Michelle, so he's been filming us walking all day through the estate. These shoes are killing me. And it's cold. We've only these cardies on, and cotton skirts. My legs are blue. Never walked so much in my whole bloody life. Blisters on my feet. I'm knackered.

The clock ticked in the background and the landlady switched on the afternoon racing for the old men in the pub. Siobhan and Michelle finished up their sandwiches and crisps and walked up the hill together towards Lazenby and Deepdale House. They stared at the blocks of flats that were earmarked for demolition. Curtains had been hung in the windows by the set dressers to make them look lived in. It was hard to differentiate what was the set and what was real.

*

The arguments began one night in the Beacon when Alan noticed Andrea sat with her back towards him. When he walked into the pub she barely acknowledged he was there. Her body language was protective, and she hunched over her drink and whispered to Pam behind her hand.

182

Alan sat opposite with his legs crossed and scribbled down a few notes for the final scene, which they were due to shoot in the coming days. *Speak to George about the ending*, he wrote. *In the play Bob's left with nothing, even sells his car. This has to be different. Bob left with a blow-up doll and note from Rita and Sue? Keep it light, keep it frothy, make em laugh. No more kitchen sink.*

As Alan wrote notes on Bob's final moments he waited to catch Andrea's attention, it was clear that she wasn't happy with some of the scenes in the film.

He stood up and put his hand on her shoulder.

She flinched and moved to one side.

What do you want? she mumbled. Can't you see I'm busy?

Can I have a word?

I don't have anything to say to you.

Andrea cocked her head to one side and pulled out the keys from her jacket pocket.

Look. This is how it is, he said. Just sit down, for one minute.

He pulled the stool away and pointed to the seat. She reluctantly shifted into the corner.

You write the script. Give it to the production company. They change it. Make it better. Add bits. Then you get paid. We add more. Take bits away. Then we shoot. And even after that we change it again. It gets butchered in the edit.

Alan gestured with his hands, holding both of his palms up towards the light.

I don't fucking care what you say. This is *my* script. I wrote it. My story. Not yours. Not anybody else's.

The anger began to rise in Andrea's voice.

That's not in dispute, he said. We know it's *your* story. But film is a different form to theatre. You've already done your part of the deal.

Thought I could trust you. I've seen what you're doing. You won't let me onto the fucking set, and you come in here, throwing your weight around. And now you're changing the ending. You've made Rita and Sue look like a right pair of slags.

Her face turned pink as the fury strangled her.

Andrea, have you ever seen my films? Gritty social realism is my middle fucking name, he said. I've spent the last ten years of my life making films about the working-class, *my class*. There is nobody else in this country right now who can do your writing justice. You have to let me do this and get it right.

His voice grated as the pub got quieter and the drinkers listened in to the flaming row that was about to erupt.

You must think I don't have a light switch on up here, Andrea said and tapped on her forehead. You've missed the point. It was always about friendship. You don't go back with someone who has rejected you. Rita and Sue would *never* go back to Bob. You've put new scenes in the script and they are a pile of fucking shit.

She picked up her handbag, cigarettes and finished her pint.

No. I'm not having it, she said.

Alan moved into the doorway and tried to block her.

This film has to be funny; I don't want to make another

depressing movie. You want to see what I'm doing next, *Road*. There's no fun in that, believe me. Nobody will want to watch this film if Bob ends up with nothing.

He shouted after her as she stormed out of the pub doorway and down the steps.

You'll thank me for this one day, he yelled. When you can buy your own house and go on holiday and every TV company in the land wants you to write for them.

Fuck off, Alan, she replied. I don't ever want to speak to you again.

*

Stayed in London last night. Patsy showed me the film first, in a cinema with ten seats. It's going to be on at Cannes with another film called Wish You Were Here. *I'm tired of it already. When I watched it all I could think about was the bits that weren't mine. And how Alan threw me off the set outside my own house. I'm upset about the ending, but there's not much we can do about that now. It's coming out soon.*

Everyone on Buttershaw wants to go and see it. They all want to watch it for free so we're going to put it on in Bradford before it comes out. Neighbours keep knocking on Mam's door asking when it's coming out. Can you get tickets for so and so. Sick to death already and it's not even released yet.

Patsy said all the newspapers will like it and see what a great writer I am. Willie, who plays Sue's Dad has got the drunk walk right down, that stagger he does. He's just like Dad, he only spent a few hours with him, so I've no idea how he managed to take him off like that.

Saw a picture of the posters that are going to be put up around Bradford, and all the cities. Some are on billboards, others are in newspapers or on bus stops. It's bright yellow and has a picture of George, Siobhan and Michelle on it. The girls wear spotty tops. Underneath it says Thatcher's Britain with Her Knickers Down. Patsy said even if some of the papers don't like it, it will all blow over in the end – and that Oscar reckons I'm the new Shelagh Delaney. Not so sure about that myself.

After the film we went to the Groucho. It was full of theatre people, like the ones at the Court. All shouting loudly and strutting around like they were famous. They double-kissed each other and wore ugly shoes. What a bunch of twats. Only members can go there. So it's a bit like Cross Lane club. Except instead of a CIU membership for a quid a year this one costs hundreds and only famous people can get in. You aren't allowed to take any pictures or ask them for autographs. I had cocktails seeing as I wasn't paying. Asked Patsy what it would be like if I brought all of Dad's mates down from the Beacon. What they'd make of it in there. Then I shouted Don't think you could get your tits out in here. She laughed at that.

The drinks came to £48. I was nearly sick when I saw the bill. Patsy paid for it with her credit card, thank God. I kept the receipt and took it home for Mam to see. She said it's more money than we have to live on in a week.

*

When *Rita, Sue and Bob Too!* made its UK premiere at Brighton Film Festival, a group of critics from the British press made the trip to watch its screening with a press conference following the film. Alan, Patsy, Sandy, Oscar, George, Siobhan and Michelle all attended the première. Andrea was nowhere to be seen. It was her twenty-sixth birthday and a night on the tiles with Eileen was on the cards. Despite the train tickets and hotel room that were booked on her behalf she snubbed the Festival and went out drinking in Bradford instead. Partly out of fear, or self-protection, Yorkshire was the only place she wanted to be that night.

Broadsheet journalists and tabloid press joined a large audience who had already heard rumours about Alan's film and its explicit material. For ninety minutes the crowd laughed, howled, and groaned at the scenes that played out in front of them. It was the first time any film had ignited such a furious response at the Festival.

The cast and crew sat on a long table after the screening as a group of journalists bayed for Andrea's blood, like ravenous hounds flushing a fox out from the ground. Some asked questions about its lack of morality and said that the film represented everything that was wrong with society. She personified the underclass, the workshy and the scroungers. The single mothers who enjoyed sex before marriage. Those on the dole who dared to get drunk. They shouted and heckled the top table, demanding an explanation for what they had just witnessed. None were familiar with Andrea's plays at the

Royal Court, but all wanted her hung, drawn and quartered for creating the filth that they had just witnessed.

Alan defended the film and Andrea's writing as journalists frantically made notes in shorthand.

I left the dialogue untouched, he said. Her writing is vibrant, alive, an authentic voice of the working-class. And yes, that *is* how people live on the Buttershaw estate.

They turned to Patsy, who stood up from her chair and almost walked out after repeated hectoring from the *Daily Express*.

I'll tell you this, she shouted. Andrea wrote about what she saw and heard around her. As depressing as it looks this is what life is like, this is how people live and talk.

A journalist put his hand up and cleared his throat.

One cannot imagine the need to create such a dreadful film, he said. It has no redeeming features, moral compass, and it contains foul language throughout. It is a disgrace that such a film has been funded by Channel 4.

How can you justify this? another asked. It has the shambolic nature of a home movie. The cast are inexperienced; Rita doesn't even have an Equity card.

The temperature in the room increased, and George drank water on the stage as the voices became louder. It was almost like facing a religious council, with the great upstanding citizens of the press passing judgment on a world they had little experience of.

How do you know what the realities are of life in the north? George said. Now, I recently played a bouncer who works at a club where girls get older men to buy them bottles of champagne for £200 and get sex as part of the deal. If I told that story to people in Bradford they'd never believe it. And it's the same for you. You blatantly know nothing about Bradford, so what makes you think we aren't telling the truth?

This is the frontline, Oscar replied. These things do happen. You don't comprehend this scenario or lifestyle because you are so far removed from it. Resignation is a way of life. Lack of aspiration and education is crippling entire communities in Yorkshire. There are estates throughout the north that have been abandoned. The set wasn't exaggerating.

Siobhan, who had remained quiet throughout the kerfuffle, leaned towards the microphone, her cheeks flushed red.

It's all well and good you saying these things about our film, she said. But when you watched *Wish You Were Here* last night you didn't complain, did you?

The room fell silent.

I mean, that's about an underage girl, carrying on with older men. That's Cynthia Payne. She's no better than Rita and Sue. Do you think because that film's set in the 1950s it makes it any better?

It's nothing to do with the time period, that's an irrelevance, a voice from the back replied.

Just because you lot remember it, that makes it acceptable, does it? Siobhan continued. But because this is happening now, in 1987, it gives you the high ground to act like the bloody Vatican.

George leaned over to Siobhan and winked. The youngest

189

person in the room had clearly won the argument. They picked up their drinks and walked to the beach.

*

The film was released in September 1987 and in the summer months following Brighton Film Festival a series of newspapers featured articles on Andrea. Lodged between comment on the general election, the Royal Family, Ian Brady's latest confession, and Jimmy Savile's new role as the saviour of Broadmoor, articles on *Rita, Sue and Bob Too!* circulated throughout the press.

THE FILM THAT TURNED A FESTIVAL BLUE
FILM KNOCKS CITY'S IMAGE
STARS DEFEND 'OFFENSIVE' FILM
LIFE'S NOT LIKE THAT AROUND HERE
LUST FOR LIFE IN SLUMLAND
FROZEN SAUSAGE FRENZY
LAND OF BLIGHTED GLORY
BONKERS IN BRADFORD
ESTATES OF THE NATION

Local journalists speculated about the content of the film in Bradford, and some reported on furious residents who were angry, despite having not seen it. It was, according to reports, an offensive sex comedy that knocked the city's image.

A photographer was dispatched to Buttershaw where a group of women were advised to look angry and hold up a newspaper to the camera. The article reported on the film's bad language and how Andrea's neighbours were demanding a confrontation with her.

We don't live like Andrea Dunbar, they said. We are *decent* people.

My daughter appeared as an extra in one of the scenes, another commented. The lack of sexual inhibitions is disgusting and now everyone thinks all of Buttershaw is like that.

Councillors were incensed and offered quotes to reporters based on a film that they hadn't even seen. The council's Policy Unit had recently invested in a tourist campaign for the city, *Bradford's Bouncing Back*, which was symbolised by a bear. The campaign was designed to counteract the city's image as the unhealthiest, and poorest, conurbation in the country. A city of unemployment, social problems, serial killers, and race protests. A man dressed in a giant bear costume wandered around outside City Hall for six months to promote the campaign's virtues. It was a sure-fire marketing idea with guaranteed results. For some, *Rita, Sue and Bob Too!* put a stop to all of their hard work.

As billboard posters appeared around the country, journalists began to harass Andrea outside her flat. They followed her friends and kerb-crawled her after last orders. Some took photographs without asking. Others called her neighbours and asked them to knock on her door. They banged on Alma's windows and offered money for contacts in the Beacon.

Articles led with details about Andrea being an unmarried mother of three children by three different fathers. Barely any acknowledged her career as a playwright. She collected the newspapers and underlined their criticism with a neon magic marker.

One afternoon Eileen called around to the flat and found her sobbing with the press cuttings laid out on the carpet in front of her.

Hey, what's all this? she said. What's the matter?

This fucking lot, that's what's the matter, Andrea said.

Don't know why you do this to yourself. Just chuck them away. Nobody cares anyway.

It's alright for you to say that, she replied. But it's not you that's being hounded.

Andrea stood up and peered through chintz curtains that framed the leaking window frame.

Look, out there. I can see him. That photographer.

Give it here, she said. Let me see. There's nobody there. Don't know what you're on about.

He is, in that car, I swear.

Andrea, he's *not* there. You need a pair of specs. Now sit down while I make you a brew.

Eileen boiled the kettle and put two teabags in each cup.

Brought Jaffa Cakes, she said. And Digestives. If I were you I'd be pleased with meself, they had queues round the block at Shipley cinema.

Huh, Andrea said. Not that I'll see any of it.

Heard that it's broke all the records, it were on the radio last night. They were talking about you, *again*.

When she walked back into the front room Andrea was crouched on all fours and started to read the articles out loud.

Sue has a way of walking typical of northern women, she said. *The lead characters are a pair of greasy-faced witches, an exercise in vulgar reality*. That's from *The Spectator*.

Stop reading them, Eileen said. Sit yourself down.

And this one, from *Mail on Sunday*, Andrea continued. I'm *a genius straight from the slums, with black teeth and a brilliant smile*. What's that meant to mean?

It doesn't mean anything, stop getting yourself wound up.

I'm hurt by that, they make me sound like I'm thick. Black teeth? Do I have black teeth?

No, of course you don't. They look white to me.

Brush em every day, twice. Don't even know why they'd write that. I've one missing, round the side.

That one that got knocked out?

Yeah, well that's why I don't smile for pictures. Cos I need to get it fixed.

But even so, they aren't black, Eileen laughed. What a thing to come out with.

I remember when she came up, the lass who wrote it. I'd been up with Andrew all night. I was exhausted, tired out. She wanted to talk about the film but I couldn't be arsed ...

Andrea slurped her tea and put a cushion on the floor; she lay back onto it and stared up at the ceiling.

That lampshade needs dusting, she said.

What happened after that?

Oh, her. She kept going on about *Wogan*, why I didn't want to go on it and be interviewed. Told her I didn't want to go on the telly. I've nowt to say.

Would've been fucking brilliant though, Eileen said. You'd have told him a thing or two . . .

That's what I was worried about. Anyway, then she banged on about New York and why didn't I go to see *The Arbor* when it was on out there.

Since when was *The Arbor* on in New York?

Oh, a few years back now, Andrea said. Must've forgotten to tell you.

Why would you forget summat like that?

Got an invite from the Mayor, you know, to fly out there. But I didn't want to fly. Can't even get in a lift, never mind an aeroplane.

So then what happened, what else did she ask you?

Jim was there, and he was pissed off that she was in the house. Said he didn't trust her. Kept asking her when she was leaving. So I told her that I don't read that many books but I like horror novels, and Caryl Churchill's plays. Then she kept asking me about this.

Andrea touched the small pink scar that bubbled on the edge of her lip.

Oh, Eileen shook her head. What did you tell her?

Shouldn't have said owt really, but it just sort of spilled out.

Told her about getting into a fight with Dad, Andrea said and started laughing. That we'd been drinking all day in the Cap and Bells then ended up brawling and I punched that woman by mistake.

Bet that went down a storm, is that the one that you punched at Easter?

Yeah, her, Pauline. The bike. Anyway, I'd been on a session wi Dad, ended up having it out with him on the front steps, then she walked into it, pulled at me from behind and fucking lamped me.

So, that all went in there, did it? Eileen said.

Yeah, the journalist wrote about it. But she got it wrong, so now it looks like I'm a thug. Told her that I don't know one person who's been in a theatre.

That's true. I mean, people only pay attention up here when it's film.

That's cos they're all too fucking lazy to read a book, going to a theatre is beyond them, Andrea said. They only watch *Gauntlet* and *Star Trek* on video round here. That's as far as it goes for most.

So, what's upsetting you? Eileen said.

This bit, in quotes: *My neighbours are the most miserable bastards in the world. They hate me because they've got nowt. But if they are attacking me they are leaving some other poor bugger alone. I can take it. This lot around here. They deserve what they get in life. Blobbin' off school, expecting everything for nothing. They'll never change their lot.*

195

Well, did you say it?

No, did I fuck. She's got it all wrong. Took what I said and made it into summat else. Now I look like a right twat, everyone's read it up here and now they all hate me.

Maybe you should get some fresh air? Let's go have a walk with the kids. Your eyes are red.

Can't go out there, Andrea said. Because they're all out to get me. And if I stay in here I've all this staring at me.

Here, let's put em away. I'll hide them somewhere, for safe keeping.

Eileen shuffled them into a box.

Shall I put em with the others? she shouted.

Yeah. Shove em in the loft. Or on the fire. Only place that's good for em.

Andrea closed the curtains and switched on the television.

I need a drink, she said.

8

Last Orders

Autumn bled into November. Red leaves clung to sycamore branches and the bright display that surrounded Shelf continued until the first snow came. Eileen hadn't visited Andrea for weeks. Letters were left unopened and the door remained locked.

Eileen had started working at the card factory, and was sent home when the electrics failed. She called into the chip shop on her way home and bought Andrea a sausage in batter and double chips with scraps from Reevy Road. They were doused in slarter and salt. Before she reached the front door Eileen had already sneaked her finger through the newspaper opening and liberated six steaming chips for the journey. The smell was unbearable.

She made her way up the path, through the main entrance,

and walked up the stairwell to the second floor. The door was left ajar. Eileen jumped over the piles of kids' shoes in the hallway; trainers, tiny wellington boots and sparkling patent leather shoes with bows and side buckles. She kicked off her boots and walked into the living room.

It's meeee! she shouted, and made her way towards the kitchen.

Washing up was piled in the sink, and the blinds were down. Eileen rummaged through the cupboards and pulled out two plates, knives and forks, and put the kettle on.

Hello! Treats are up.

Her voice echoed through the flat.

There was no reply. Eileen shouted again and unloaded a mountain of chips onto the plates and poured out two mugs of tea. She opened the kitchen door and stuck her head out, calling Andrea's name. Toys were scattered in the back garden. A pair of sparrows hung from a bird feeder, fighting each other for soft nuts.

Eileen washed her greasy hands in the sink and pushed the doors open around the flat. Andrea was under the covers, in bed.

Eh. What's up? What you doin in ere ...

Eileen sat on the edge of the bed and put her hand on Andrea's hip.

Nowt, she replied. Just can't get up, that's all.

Bundles of washing formed mounds in each corner of the room. Talcum powder made a film on the glass-top dresser and a framed print of Pearson's *Wings of Love* hung over the bed. Andrea pulled the sheet over her head and turned her back.

But I've brought chips.

Eileen walked around the other side of the bed and plonked her bum next to Andrea's face.

They're well nice today. And a sausage. Know how much you like em.

Don't feel like it.

Andrea shifted away as Eileen tried to give her a hug.

Please. Just go, she said. I can't cope with owt today.

We could have em up here, Eileen laughed. I got scraps and everything. And ketchup. We could eat em in bed. Your new fella would love that, wouldn't he?

A secret smile appeared on Andrea's face. Eileen could see the gap in her teeth on the side and heard a chuckle from the covers.

Right, Eileen said. Well that's decided then ...

She ran down the corridor and balanced both plates on a tray, with the mugs of tea squashed together and rattled her way back to the bedroom. Eileen made a pillow nest and pulled Andrea up, making a nest for the two of them.

Let's watch some telly, she said.

After turning the dial three times and shifting the coat-hanger aerial into various positions she tuned in to a gameshow repeat. It blared in the corner of the room as Andrea reluctantly ate a few chips and slurped the cooling brew; her hands shook as she sipped.

I haven't eaten for days, Andrea croaked. Stomach's shrivelled up.

I know that. You look white as a sheet.

Eileen sucked on her fingers and crunched a giant scrap of batter between her teeth.

I'd have come round before if knew you were this bad, she said.

Andrea pointed to a pile of envelopes on the windowsill. Her eyes were sore and puffy. She rubbed them and scratched her scalp.

Were supposed to be in London today. BBC wanted me to write a play. Sent me train tickets. Writing's too hard. Don't even like doing it . . . can't concentrate anywhere but the pub . . . can't cope with the kids . . . it's all . . . getting on top of me . . .

Eileen sat up and opened the blinds, letting the bright afternoon light beam onto the bed.

Nobody's making you. There's other things you can do aside from writing. Bit of sun'll do you the world of good.

The sun's rays hit a crimson velvet dress that hung in a bag from the drycleaners, and illuminated the diamantes on its shoulder pads. Dust particles floated through the air. The dress had been purchased from T J Hughes for the opening of *Rita, Sue and Bob Too!* in Brighton, the event Andrea never made. She left it hanging on the end of the wardrobe, a constant reminder of what might have been.

Eileen lifted the wire hanger up and buried it beneath the coats.

You can put that dress away, for starters. No use wallowing, she added. There'll be chance to wear it another day.

*

It was supposed to be a chance to patch things up. During the previous months day leaked into night and night bled into day. Andrea and Jim's arguments escalated, they were explosive. Broken crockery, stiletto heels, scratches and yelps. The rage descended. Bin-bags full of clothes were packed and emptied and the kids spent more time with Alma as the year went on.

The royalties Andrea received from the film were spent on things she never had the money to buy; fitted carpets for the bedrooms, a shower, locks for the front door, August holidays to Scarborough for the kids. The rest was spent in the pub.

David disparagingly called her new friends 'kling-ons', the ones who followed her around asking if she could stump them a pint. She never refused. Andrea was generous. What was hers was everybody else's. It seemed only fair, considering her best material was gleaned from listening in to their conversations. *Shirley* had come about the same way, from overhearing gossip about a friend of a friend.

Long afternoons were spent watching people, how they spoke, their reactions, relationships, moods. That was the whole part of the job of being a writer. Observing other people, what they were doing and more importantly what they *weren't* doing. Their business was her business. Before the kids came home from school she'd walk back to the flat and write everything down she'd heard in the pub, word for word. People started warning others not to talk to her. They called her Enid Blyton.

Don't sit next to her, they said. You'll be in her next story . . .

A friend of Alma's picked up the children from school every afternoon, and brought them to the Beacon for half three. They drank lemonade, ate packets of crisps, coloured in, and played dominos on the round tables in the Tap Room. At half six she walked them back to the flat and cooked tea. It was the same routine every day.

It was hard living on her own again but Jim still called in on her every week, just to check she was coping. He suggested a night out together in town. No hangers-on, no distractions. It had been months since they spent any time with each other. He offered to book a taxi and collected her from Alma's in the afternoon. They drank a couple of tinnies in her back garden with a drop of vodka in the top and christened the new drink 'turbos'. The perfect start to the night.

Andrea wore her light jacket, high shoes, white blouse and perfume, and as they piled into the back of the taxi Jim grabbed hold of her tiny waist and stroked her tawny coloured hair.

You've scrubbed up well, he said. Let's have a good one today. Leave everything else behind us.

Lorraine promised to feed Lisa with microwave meals that Andrea had left in the freezer for lunch. She left a pile of coins for sweets on the sideboard. Lorraine was responsible for her age. At nine years old she had the prettiest face, by far the best looking girl on Buttershaw.

Not many girls were mixed-race on the estate, in fact she may have been the only one. Lorraine had her father's colouring. Yousaf had barely shown any interest in her, but one day he appeared and took her out for the afternoon. He brought her back in the car wearing traditional Pakistani dress. He'd bought her a bright pink salwar kameez from Bombay Stores. After he left Andrea cut it to pieces with her kitchen scissors. She shouted that she didn't want a daughter of hers wearing clothes like that.

Lorraine cried for a week afterwards.

Jim and Andrea asked the taxi to head to City Vaults, by the Wool Exchange. They planned to walk through town, towards the Unicorn, have a couple in the Pack Horse then up to the City Gent. They would pace themselves. Eat something on the way. Jim promised not to sing when they walked through the doors of the Boy & Barrel, but couldn't help himself when the backing track began to play *Everlasting Love*. Jim took to the microphone in the half-empty pub.

Andrea could hear him singing from the Ladies and refused to come out until he stopped. When she glimpsed through the crack in the door Jim had re-created Elvis's Las Vegas for the Westgate regulars and thrashed out a series of karate moves at the crescendo beneath the big screen. Disco lights flashed around the room and an old man danced with an imaginary partner around him. A group of men slumped over their pints, staring into the abyss. The barmaid rolled a cigarette and winced at Jim as he tried to reach the high notes. Andrea was not impressed.

As they wandered up to the Beehive by Lumb Lane, she began to feel queasy. They had managed not to argue all day, and Jim was being attentive. They played pool together and reminisced, put *Silly Games* on the jukebox three times in a row, just like the good old days. The bitterness held back. But she could taste a sickness in her mouth, and felt more drunk than usual. She drank a glass of water to steady herself and Jim found her sat outside on her own getting some air.

By the time they reached the bottom of Great Horton Road, Andrea was plastered. She remembered Jim eating a tray of chips and staggering through the traffic at the crossroads. She remembered needing to piss and going round the back of the dustbins, where a rat skittered out across the cobblestones.

After that it was only a feeling. The temper rising through her veins, her shouting and falling on the road and both of them clinging to each other on the pavement and Jim picking her up as she pulled him down and the red lights flashing on / off in the background and everything slipping and her eyes doubling up and her body collapsing through the big glass porch at Jim's house.

She didn't remember getting back to the flat.

Or Lorraine trying to clean the blood off the carpet.

Or the shards of glass that were lodged in her cheeks.

Or the ambulance ride to Bradford Infirmary.

But she did remember the lights and the rage. The heat in her veins. The crack when her head had smashed through the door. And even worse, when she held a mirror up, her skin black and blue from the fall, sixty stitches held one side of her face together. Zigzags and sutures, threads and knots, scabs and sores and leaks. The left side was swollen, and her eye bloodshot from the night before. The doctors told her she would have to eat through a straw. They gave her a transfusion, two pints of blood. Her left wrist was hooked to a catheter; a central line fed her type O from a bag.

A lump on her temple throbbed.

She told the doctors she remembered nothing.

*

A court summons arrived in early December. The letter, hand delivered and signed for by Alma, had a red stamp on the front. It was sent by the Magistrates' Court and contained information about a case filed against Andrea by the Department of Health and Social Security. She had tried her hardest to ignore it but it didn't take them long to find her on the electoral roll.

It was another bleak winter's day. Snow coated the hill tops and the icy wind dragged on the back of her calves as she climbed onto the bus into town. Alma and Andrea both wore their court clothes. Smart skirt and blouse. Polished shoes. Wool overcoat. It was important to look presentable, despite the inevitable. They walked through the salt-scuffed streets by the Alhambra; the ochre spots of grit splattered on their shoes, and they crossed over the ring road towards the court. Lorries loaded with fallen stock drove past on their way to the glue factory. Car engines rattled and buses spewed diesel fumes into the air. Wet tyres fizzed against the asphalt.

Andrea rubbed her hands together to warm them up, and pulled out her lighter and packet of Sovereigns in the foyer. Beneath the shelter discarded butts were trampled into concrete, leftovers from the morning's case, a hundred discarded thoughts. She was due to appear in an hour.

Miserable today, Andrea said. No change in town, then.

She looked up over the road towards the National Museum of Photography, Film and Television. A large statue of J.B. Priestley surveyed the ring road. Underneath his looming body, gargantuan and cast in bronze, the words AUTHOR and O.M. were chiselled in the granite plinth. Bradford's greatest literary achievement. A playwright the city could be proud of. A legacy for tourists. A face to plaster on the side of buses. Balding and chunky, dressed in a smart suit and coat. John Boynton Priestley, Order of Merit. Manningham lad made good.

Keep thinking about Sundays, Mam. When we were kids.

Andrea pointed towards a tower block where a sign for ICE SKATING flickered on the tenth floor.

Dad took us in there, all of us. We went skating every week. It were great.

Not for long though, Alma laughed. We couldn't afford it.

But you did love it. Made you happy. You allus slept like logs on Sundays. It were a blessing.

She lit her cigarette in the howling wind as Alma held up her coat.

I remember . . . only a few years back. This woman were on the rink. Had her little lass with her, showing her how to skate. Dad were on the ice with the girls. I watched them wobbling about from the sides . . .

Oh, is this the one that fell?

Yeah. They had this big tannoy playing music. And they put on that Torvill and Dean song. The woman, well, she were a big woman, and anyway, she had this long dress on and started doing circles on the ice. Her little lass were clinging to the side, wouldn't let go. Her Mam said 'Look, this is how you do it, cross your legs, move into it.' And I could see what were coming . . .

Andrea shuffled to one side as two policemen walked up the steps with clipboards.

The music played loud, she continued. Like on the Olympics. And then there were a scream, and then she fell. I saw her, there, wailing on the rink.

Poor woman, Alma shook her head. What a place to fall.

Do you know what the worst thing was? Nobody helped her and everyone laughed. Even I fucking laughed. The whole place roared. And she were just layin there. It were funny but I still feel bad about it. Think she broke her leg.

Andrea rummaged around in her coat, dug out a sweet and sucked on it.

Lots of things I feel bad about, she said. Must be clocking em up.

Do you think we best be going in? Alma asked. It's nearly twelve.

She took Andrea's arm and they walked towards the check-in desk, where their bags were searched. The floor was patterned with Burmantofts tiles which shone in oxblood and black beneath hanging lamps. Andrea walked up the double staircase, and ran her hands along the polished banister that reflected her face. They headed towards the back of the large waiting room where a desk with a sign for DUTY SOLICITOR overlooked the seats. The waiting room led into eight separate rooms, and sweating defendants sat in silence outside each court waiting for their time to come. Andrea could smell the fear.

Never gets any easier, coming in here, she said. Waiting for court sitting to flash up, it's like time stands still.

Not long now, love, Alma replied. Look, that's the solicitor. Shall we collar him?

They walked into Court 6 and Andrea sat on the front bench as Alma watched from a few rows back. A reporter scribbled in shorthand and a secretary typed up notes from the prosecutor. A barrister represented the DHSS.

Andrea was asked to confirm her name, address, date of birth and marital status. They charged her with non-declaration of income despite correspondence dating back five years. The judge read a statement from the prosecutors who believed that she had recently earned money from a film, which had not been declared. She had continued to claim her giro and housing benefit.

The barrister read from a series of documents as Andrea turned her head towards Alma, who nodded back at her. When they asked Andrea to make a statement on the witness stand she walked slowly up the steps and swore to tell the truth as she placed her hand on a black King James Bible.

It's not my fault, she told them. I didn't know I had to declare money. And even if I did, I wouldn't know how to. I haven't received any royalties yet. But I did earn £5,400 from my giro last year. It's been a rough year for me.

She faced the jury and showed them the deep scars behind her hair.

Look at my face, she said. I had to have plastic surgery this year. Fell through a glass door.

Is that what you've spent your money on? the prosecution asked.

Yeah, she said and looked away. Had to get it sorted out. I've faced a series of blows in my life. In my mind I've been saying I'm going to give the writing up. It's something I have to think over.

The court fell silent. Andrea cleared her throat and turned to the judge, who peered over his half-glasses.

I regret ever starting to write for all the trouble it's brought me, she said. People think I'm rich. But I'm not. I've got nothing. I have to live with my parents and my three children. I'm twenty seven years old. Don't know where my next money is coming from.

The solicitor interjected and showed paperwork to the panel, confirming her financial problems. He added that the money she had earned from the film had been spent on expenses, travelling to London and staying in hotels. She was due to receive royalties from the film as a percentage in 1989. Like the characters she portrayed in her plays, Andrea was living in extreme poverty.

The judge wrote down a series of figures and delivered a verdict that she would pay back the £5,400 at £3 a week with £75 costs and a £50 fine. She listened to him speak and took considerable pleasure in the knowledge it would take thirty-four years to pay the government its money back.

*

Ice outside. They've been filming up here this week. Yorkshire Television this time. Man called Mike, a producer. Asked me to write something new for a programme he's making. Said it's called the Great North Show. *They're calling this episode* In Praise of Bad Girls. *Tomorrow's at Theatre in the Mill. Filmed the bell tower yesterday and the light coming on at the Beacon. The kids leaving school. I've nothing to say. Even writing this is hard. My hands are shaking.*

They've got Tony's drama group reading The Arbor *out loud. And me watching from the seats. Like that* Arena, *where it all began. I am tired. Tried to write for it. A new piece. Tried but couldn't. Sent it to Mike. Five times. He said he couldn't read it. That it didn't make sense. He couldn't tell if it was a monologue or just thoughts in my head. Asked me if I could type it up but told him I don't have a typewriter so just sent him the pages from a pad. Kay is acting in it. She's alright. Grew up on an estate in Leeds. Bit like here. Said she wrote for* Coronation Street. *Reckons I should be writing again.*

Mike keeps ringing the pub. Leaving messages for me. Then Kay turned up one day. Found me in the Tap Room. Said she'd rung every pub in Bradford trying to find me. Kept asking if everything was alright. That I looked frail. Said I could talk to her. That she knew what it was like. Trying to write and not being able to. Told her I've not been well. Can't even finish a scene. Or think of what to say. All that stuff in my head, the lines. They're gone. As if someone emptied my brain and nothing replaced what was in there.

Not been the same since I fell.

Hope it comes back. That thing I once had.

Kay said Mike wanted to finish this film. That she would write it for me if I want. Told her I'd already been paid and spent the money. She said that didn't matter. That they'd put my name on the credits and pretend I'd written it.

Had a smoke with her outside. Said as long as I could read it first that was alright. We went back inside and she wrote some lines down and read them. Sounded enough like me, nobody will notice.

Then I told her what I'd been thinking.

That I don't want to work with men again.

211

I've had enough of them.

So Kay's going to help make the film. Says she'll drive me into town.

My head hurts.

*

In Andrea's last interview, she sat on a stool in a darkened room and smoked as the lights caught the wisps of nicotine rising from her lips. The camera filmed her from one side, her scars hidden in the shadows.

Do I look like an alcoholic as well as a chain smoker? she laughed, as the reels started running.

The programme opened with footage of Andrea working on a production line at ASJ. She was earning money for Christmas packing boxes at a warehouse in Buttershaw. Each morning Andrea walked up from the estate towards Beacon Road and clocked onto a shift at Mandale Mill. Her giro had been stopped after the court case and it was the only way she could support herself. Her mother, brothers and sisters all worked there and offered to split their shifts with her. She had spent the past two months packing luxury stereo systems into bubble-wrap before sending them off to penthouse suites with London postcodes.

As a child she had always imagined she would appear on the television; that was her goal. Since she had been on the screen her dreams had dissolved. There was nothing left to hope for.

From Buttershaw to Bowling Mill to London, the cinema and back to the factory floor. No words left to write. Just the grind and dimming light of rattling mill. Everything in the past. Her fame a distant memory.

As the camera began to film, Kay asked her questions about *The Arbor*, how it first arrived at the Royal Court.

The Arbor was about me . . . it was a lot easier than I thought it would be, she said. I suppose cos it were getting done in London, maybe I wanted it to work. I had so much in me it *had* to work.

Andrea supped on a can of beer and answered the questions about Buttershaw slowly.

I like the area because that's all I've ever known. It's no better or worse than anywhere else, she continued. It certainly isn't as bad as some people make it out to be. You don't have to be hard to live around here. You've just got to have a knowledge of working-class life. Even from me moving to Buttershaw, it's allus had a bad name. And I don't find it that bad at all. I moved away, a few times, but I can't resist coming back. I dunno, I just like the people so much around here.

What about the film? Kay asked. Are you proud of what you wrote?

After the first draft they got another writer to do it, she said. By that time I'd lost interest, I'll be honest with you. I was so pissed off with the carrying on, bringing other writers in and everything, that I thought I'd start another. So I wrote *Shirley*.

What was it that upset you about the film?

I wanted it to concentrate on the friendship between them two but not really on the other characters. But not so much like a couple of slappers and what they get up to. I don't look at my characters as slags, just because they've been with a man before they find the right one, doesn't mean to say they are slags. I mean, nobody would look on it like that in middle-class backgrounds, but if it's working-class they get called slags. I don't see it like that at all ...

Andrea's voice drifted as a clank of a motorbike engine started up in the distance.

Kay shuffled her notes and Andrea wandered around the empty theatre, before sitting down again.

I've got a few more things to say, she said. I love this, the theatre. Being in here. Much prefer theatre to film. Cinema has too much space.

She pointed at the floorboards and the curtain above them.

On a stage you see more, she said. You can *say* more. Once a film director gets hold of it, you have no say. But then again I've got to see it how I want to see it. And not as *they* do. I need that. My view, not their view ...

How do you see the role of women in your plays? Kay added. Would you call yourself a feminist?

I have been asked a lot of times if I am a feminist. I don't think of myself as a feminist writer. Maybe I think of myself as a *straight writer*, Andrea laughed. I wouldn't say I was a feminist ... but, I must admit, I like women to be stronger than men. I don't know why, it's just the way I write.

214

After the interview ended the crew took Andrea for a drive around the estate in a hatchback saloon, and filmed her with her wavy hair blowing in the wind. Behind her the houses flashed by. She waved at a couple of lads out trotting towards the Boulevard as the cameras rolled, their painted carts wobbling as the horses' hooves ricocheted off slushy tarmac. Snow covered the roofs, cars and gardens and a salmon pink light cloaked the estate. The street lamps trembled on as the winter sun sank beneath the clock tower.

*

After the screening of *In Praise of Bad Girls*, Kay kept in contact with Andrea. There was still no agent to represent her, yet Kay visited her on the estate, often with words of encouragement. Throughout 1989 she made trips to Buttershaw, in the various flats and houses Andrea lived in, and suggested ideas to her. Producers, agents, theatres. Andrea still couldn't write. And even if she did, the words didn't fit together. She was paralysed by writer's block.

One of Andrea's ideas was based on a gang of debt collectors. The twisted, violent and manipulative men who sometimes drank in the Beacon. The residents had lookouts on the estate, and if the moneylender's car was spotted word quickly spread via their children who dashed up the road on their bicycles.

Some of Andrea's neighbours arranged a time and date for

visits and moved their furniture next door so there was nothing left to repossess when they walked into the house. Others draped double sets of net curtains at the window, so the debt collectors couldn't see into the living rooms from outside. It was a game of cat and mouse. The henchmen knew every trick in the book, but the inventive reasons and excuses for not paying back their washing machine debt, often at 500% interest, never failed to delight Andrea. Kay knew of moneylenders on Ireland Wood who used similar brutal tactics. Both agreed it would make a good story.

Andrea told Kay she was working on a new script which was set in the Beacon, and was a follow-up to *Rita, Sue and Bob Too*. It would contain similar characters.

It's all in my head, she said. But it's still too noisy for me to concentrate on writing at home. I've nowhere to write and nothing to write on.

After a series of calls to Bradford Council Kay told Andrea she had arranged an office for her to use in the centre of town, if she wanted it. It was a bit cold and the décor was basic but there was a word processor.

No good to me, she remarked. Don't even know how to switch the machine on, never mind type on it.

The room remained empty.

In January Kay was invited to appear on a panel at Riverside Studios, in Hammersmith, about working-class female writers in film and television. The organisers offered her a fee, hotel and travel to London overnight and Kay suggested that

Andrea would be a far better person to appear. They told her they had considered it but had no way of reaching her. Kay agreed to twist Andrea's arm and contacted her the following day via the pub's telephone.

No. I'm not bloody doing it, Andrea said.

Why? I'll come with you. They're paying good money. We'll go together.

What am I going to say? They'll expect me to be a dancing monkey. I don't like talking.

You'll be brilliant, Kay added. You don't need them, but they need you. Think about it. You've got the upper hand.

The organisers sent a pair of first class rail tickets to Kay's house in Leeds and reluctantly Andrea agreed to appear. They would meet at Leeds Station at 8am and catch the train together down to King's Cross. There was no guarantee that Andrea would turn up, but Kay was insistent that she made the trip. It would do her good. Help her confidence.

At 1am, five hours before Kay was due to get up to catch her train, the phone rang in the downstairs hallway. Kay ignored it and let it ring. Once, twice, three times.

Who the hell is that? Kay grumbled as she pulled on her slippers and dressing gown, and picked up the phone, as the answering machine flashed up a series of messages.

Hello. Leeds, Mellor, she said. An operator interjected with reverse charges.

It's me. A voice wobbled on the end of the line.

Andrea? What time is it? Are you alright? Kay sat down on

217

the carpeted stairs and ran her fingers through her long dark hair which had knotted down her back.

No. It's all gone to shit. I'm not coming tomorrow.

Andrea sounded hoarse; her words barely audible down the line.

Been at it all night, she said. Went for him. Got out of hand.

Are you sure . . . you don't want me to come and get you?

No. I'm alright but I can't come to London, she paused. You go without me.

What's wrong? Kay asked. I know it's late. But you can tell me. You know that.

Can't talk right now. Have to go. I'm sorry. Didn't mean to let you down.

Andrea's voice was replaced by a buzz and the line disconnected. It wasn't the first time Andrea had called her late, but she sounded more disturbed than usual. Kay barely slept all night. Her guts were still churning as the alarm rang at 6am.

Kay drove into Leeds Station, parked up and carried her small overnight bag into the foyer. She bought a copy of the *Yorkshire Post* from the kiosk. Her train was due at 8.10am. She stood on the windy platform, stared up the departures board and felt a tap on her shoulder.

Morning, a voice said.

It was Andrea.

What the hell are you doing here? Kay laughed. Thought you'd be dead to the world after last night's carrying on.

Thought I should come after all. No point wallowing.

She looked smaller and more fragile than ever. Wearing her tight jeans, white stilettos and bomber jacket, she stumbled into the first class carriage with Kay.

Never been first class, Andrea said. Normally in the cheap seats . . .

They sat down in the carriage and removed their coats.

Your neck . . . it looks sore.

Kay put her fingers to her own neck, moving them around her throat in gentle circles.

Don't want to talk about it, Andrea murmured.

She stared into Kay's eyes. They were bloodshot from the night before.

Andrea sat down with her handbag on her lap, took a deep breath and played with the serviette in front of her. She turned it into a paper aeroplane, ready to be thrown from a great height.

Kay ordered a pot of tea from the waiter and started to read through a pile of notes in her bag. *Band of Gold* and a question mark was scrawled across the top.

Let's have some breakfast, Kay said. We get a Full English in this carriage. Like royalty.

Don't want owt. I've got some mints. They'll do.

Andrea stared out across Leeds as the Intercity 125 darted towards Wakefield.

I'll have a beer though.

It's only half eight, Kay added. Isn't it a bit early?

Never too early. I like an early drink, me.

The waiter put a hot teapot on the table and laid out silver cutlery in front of Kay. He unfolded a cotton napkin across her lap and brought a cooked breakfast under a metallic lid, which he lifted out in front of her.

Ugh. Don't know how you can eat that.

Andrea turned her nose up at Kay's food. Mind if I smoke?

The carriage was packed with businessmen dressed in pinstripe suits reading the broadsheets and making notes with fountain pens. They scrolled through their Filofaxes. Their briefcases were stuffed with official documents as they talked about Labour's 12% lead over the Conservatives and what a huge financial disaster it would be if that odious ginger Welshman got into power.

Kay and Andrea listened in and sniggered at the Received Pronunciation that permeated the carriage.

Eh, we shouldn't be in here, should we? Kay remarked. Do you think they'll find us out?

Andrea opened a can of lager and poured it straight down her throat, spilling drops onto her top and jeans. She let out a manly belch as the coffee pot steamed behind the counter. The rest of the carriage tutted and the businessmen glared as they shook the folds in their pink newspapers.

That should take the edge off, she said. I'm nervous about tonight.

Well don't be, Kay added. I've got your back. It'll be alright. If they ask you something complicated all you have to say is 'I don't understand, can you please explain it again?'

But they'll all be snooty. Up their own arses. They all think I'm thick down there.

Andrea, you are *not* thick. You're one of the smartest women I've ever met. Don't say that because it's not true.

Kay pushed a third piece of toast into her mouth and picked off a strand of marmalade that had stuck to the side of her chin.

I do know, you know, Andrea said and kicked Kay's feet under the table.

I know you do, she replied.

*

A Hackney Cab pulled up outside the Imperial Hotel on Russell Square and Kay and Andrea jumped out onto the pavement as cars, motorbikes and buses rattled past the building. The air was thick with fumes and swarms of people raced between the traffic as the lights turned red. Andrea refused to board the Underground at King's Cross, being a hundred feet below made her feel claustrophobic. Both agreed to take a taxi to Hammersmith that night, and would make the event organiser foot the bill.

Andrea hadn't brought a change of clothes, but had a spare pair of knickers in her handbag. Kay offered to lend her deodorant, a squirt of Red Door, concealer and lipstick. Their rooms were situated on the eighth floor. Kay walked towards the lift across the busy reception which bustled with teams of

American tourists out in London for a West End show. Andrea stopped in front of the doors. Not going in there, she said.

What? Kay laughed. It's only a lift. We won't get stuck.

Not getting in a fucking lift, Kay. Aren't being funny or owt but it's not happening. We have to walk.

It's eight floors up. Can't you just shut your eyes for a few seconds and think about something else?

You do what you want . . .

Andrea disappeared through the double doors and started trudging up the carpeted steps.

Wait on. I'll come with you.

Kay picked up her case and chased her up the stairwell.

After a few hours asleep face-down on the bed, Andrea woke to a banging at the door. Kay had come to collect her for the event. The mini-bar was already empty and Andrea drank a cup of tea as the night began to twinkle over the towers of Goodge Street. She pointed at the Post Office Tower, the highest building in town.

Couldn't live here. Do my head in, she mumbled as she tried to open the window. Can't even get the windows open in this place. I'm sweating.

Her groans about the city continued all the way to Riverside Studios, as they crawled through the gridlock past the Houses of Parliament and on towards Chelsea Bridge. The Thames glittered against the Christmas lights that were still left over from the previous month. It was 1990, the start of a new decade.

Andrea coughed grey flecks into her handkerchief, scrunched it up and put it in her bag. She pointed towards the stucco-fronted townhouses that lined the road.

Thing is, she said. What I don't get about London, how come all the buildings are nice? Nothing looks shit. Look, out there. Everything's white. In West Yorkshire all the stone is black, the muck clings to it. Even the bad bits down here look like palaces compared to Bradford.

The taxi wound its way through the back streets until they arrived at the studios. A sign saying SOLD OUT was pinned to the door and a queue of people waited outside the auditorium. Andrea waited around the corner and talked into Kay's ear.

I'm not going in there. Not until they've gone in, she said.

Inside the studio a crowd of two hundred people jostled and chattered as Kay and Andrea watched from the Green Room upstairs. Antonia, another writer, gave Kay a hug when she walked into the room. They cracked open a bottle of wine and tried to calm Andrea's nerves before they went on.

It was the first time Andrea had appeared in public, but Kay was convinced she'd rise to the occasion.

It will be fine, she told her. The crowd are interested in what you have to say. If they ask a hard question ask them to repeat it in a way that everyone can understand. Have some faith in yourself.

When Andrea finally walked out onto the stage the audience clapped and whooped. The light beamed onto her and she could barely see out against the glare. Some shouted her name. The audience were there to hear her speak. As the host began his introductions Andrea stood up, picked up her handbag and walked off the stage. The audience rustled. Kay leaned over to Antonia. Neither had any idea why she had left the event. Both presumed it was stage fright.

Ten minutes later Andrea reappeared and strutted across the stage with a glass of water. The room fell silent.

Sorry, she said. Just been to the lav!

The crowd burst into laughter. And for the next forty-five minutes Andrea answered every question astutely. No stone left unturned. Then the audience were given a microphone. Most wanted to talk to Andrea, she was clearly the star attraction.

A tall man wearing a leather coat and Mission t-shirt spoke first.

In light of the recent government's cuts to social security, he said. Do you have an opinion on the dismantling of the welfare state?

Well, if you're talking about dole then yes, I do have an opinion. Let's put it this way, Andrea coughed on the microphone. There aren't enough hours in the day to explain my views on Mrs Thatcher.

Another voice spoke from the crowd, a well-spoken woman wearing theatrical clothes.

Can I ask what your position is on the Asian community of Bradford, she said. Your first play went into some detail on the issue but I am curious to hear if your views have changed in recent years?

I don't know what you mean by *position*, she answered. But I'll tell you this, there are a lot of problems in Bradford and most of it comes down to lack of money. I'm not a racist and I have a half-caste child. I know a lot about Pakistanis, lived with one for a while. For me *The Arbor* wasn't about race at all . . . it was about useless men.

The audience laughed.

I mean it, she continued. Doesn't matter what colour they are, they're all the bloody same.

Hi, a young woman waved from the audience. I'm Sally.

Hello Sally, she replied. You might need to speak up, can't hear you.

I want to be a writer and I grew up on a council estate a bit like yours, the microphone buzzed. I find it really hard to get work or find out where I can put my plays on. Can you give me any advice?

Andrea laughed and crossed her legs.

I'm the last person you should be asking for advice. This has been the hardest thing I've ever done. Writing is a grind. You see me here on this stage and think I've made it. The reality is different.

What do you mean by that? the girl said.

It's not what it's cracked out to be. You make money, but you spend it. Then you're back to square one again, Andrea paused. I struggle all the time, even now. Can't get owt finished, can't come up with ideas. Kay knows all about that, don't you Kay?

Kay nodded at Andrea from across the stage.

I stumbled on writing by accident. It found me. Like it's found you. But if you come from an estate then you'll always be an outsider in this world, she gestured to the stalls in the theatre. As long as you're alright with that then there's no reason you won't succeed.

As the event wound up Andrea answered the questions that other panellists struggled to complete. Her lucidity astonished the audience of television producers, commissioners and agents, so much so that by the time the event ended she was besieged by offers of work and representation.

Well-heeled Londoners with middle-class accents shook her hand and told her how delightful she was. They pushed their business cards into her palm and offered to buy her drinks.

I hate these cunts, she said to Kay in the bar afterwards. They're all so false. Can't be doing with em at all. They never say what they mean.

*

Red and orange lights flickered through net curtains as the crackle and pop of old tyres, hissing damp wood and exploding aerosol cans raged against the heat of the fire. It wasn't bonfire night, but there was enough litter on the Arbor's verges to justify a burn up. The kids built one every few months, after the council had stopped cleaning the streets. Buttershaw was the least of their priorities. Teenagers and children gathered around spitting flames and sprawled their bodies in the grass, staring at the sky above them.

It was a clear, cloudless night and towards the east the summer triangle glimmered in the distance. The crescent moon rested above the rooftops and kids sucked on doffed cigarettes, chased their friends around the rampaging fire. Litre bottles of cherry pop were shared out, each child belching louder than the last. The older lads smoked spliffs by the roadside. Girls gathered in groups and sat on the redbrick wall which over-looked the Arbor. Most had permed hair, with heavily sprayed fringes and wore loose, baggy jeans, Kickers with Grolsch tops, and Avon make-up pancaked on their cheeks.

Andrea sat in Alma's living room and listened to the babble outside. She could hear a sickly rendition of *I Think We're Alone Now* from the wall and the boys' laughter as one of the girls tripped over a broken kerb. One of them had been sucking adhesive from a canister and plastic bag and ran screaming along the footpath convinced that the stars were a hundred thousand arrows trying to impale him. His face was covered in glue-spots. Lorraine was playing outside with her friends. Lisa sat on the sun-lounger on the patio, blowing giant bubbles into the night. Andrew was asleep at his Dad's house.

Inside the living room a heap of carrier bags was scattered on the patterned carpet, one contained the screenplay drafts for *Rita, Sue and Bob Too!* Alma had pulled them out from underneath the bed as she was redecorating the room. The wallpaper and posters that had been there since her childhood were steam-stripped, and piled up in mounds by the side of the house, their paper trails spilling into the garden. Alma found drawings, scribbles and bubble gum behind Andrea's single bed that had been there since they first moved to Buttershaw.

Old diaries, letters, and negatives were buried in the bags. Pictures of Andrea and Tony outside a Hall of Mirrors at Blackpool Pleasure Beach on Feast Week; both holding baby monkeys, dressed in tiny knitted jumpers and bright red suits. A school photograph from Horton Bank Top Junior School was paper-clipped to a school report, where a nine-year-old Andrea beamed brightly, dressed in a cardigan and blouse. Another was taken by Eileen outside the refuge, where Andrea leaned to one side, dressed in a pair of navy culottes, an open-necked turquoise lapelled shirt, light tights and wedge sandals.

She sifted through the remnants of her past; at photos, teenage diaries and love letters that she had once squirreled away. Letters from Craig, who had drawn a heart in felt tip on the top of the page, her sister Kathy had scribbled over the top writing HAHAHA when he told her that he loved her. She obviously hadn't hidden them well enough. Some of the drafts from *The Arbor* were still in the same bag that she had carried with her to the refuge. And notes, in green biro, on lined paper, with the first patches of dialogue for *Rita*.

Andrea pulled out the screenplay and sat in John Brian's

comfy chair, the smell of his hair wax embedded in the upholstery. She looked at the words and replayed the film in her head.

Another bag contained a pile of cuttings that Alma had collected. Articles and interviews with her. Pictures torn from the *Sunday Times*, with Andrea dressed in white outside Alma's old flat on Sloan Square, in the centre of Bradford, just before it was demolished. Photographers always wanted her to pose against run-down buildings or outside boarded-up houses on the estate.

The mirror had started reflecting another person's face, her father's. She was frightened she was becoming him. His drinking, his mouth, the way he walked. The trouble he brought, the restless gait. Even the Beacon's drinkers said *you're getting more like your father every day.*

Sleepless nights, stress, and three children hadn't improved her lot. Still, her eyes were bluer than the sea, and even after having the children she still fitted into her tight jeans. That was something to celebrate, at the very least.

The script and her notes were piled on the oval coffee table. Andrea picked up her pen and began to scribble over the words. Scrawled her biro over every page, and crumpled the paper into balls. The carriage clock struck its bell.

I can't do this, she whispered. Just. Too. Much.

Andrea gathered her papers together and walked, barefoot towards the door. The afternoon drinking made her unstable, but she knew what needed to be done. The long grass stroked the backs of her ankles as she walked towards the blazing fire on the far side of the Arbor.

Lorraine called to her, but she continued walking, baby steps at first. And wished the fire could eat her. Men's faces appeared in the inferno, shapes she recognised from the past; Yousaf, Mick, Jim, Craig, Max, Alan, John Brian. All faces became one. The scent of alcohol ran through her pores, its sickly sweet smell now familiar.

There was no escaping what she had written. She wondered what burning to death felt like, and if that was easier than the life she had lived. Andrea stopped in front of the bonfire as the heat curled the mascara on her eyelashes, and felt a nettle rash rise up her feet. She emptied the carrier bags from under her arms and cremated the pages in the pit.

Sources

Prologue

The Arbor. (2010). [film] UK: Clio Barnard.

'*Bad points: feel very emotional ... Want the kids to be okay*' Gardner, L. (1998). Born to Write and Die. *The Guardian.* 04/07/98.

The Great North Show: In Praise of Bad Girls. (1989). [TV programme]. Yorkshire TV. 31/01/89.

Hargreaves, J.A. (2004). Dunbar, Andrea (1961-1990). *Oxford Dictionary of National Biography.* Oxford University Press.

Johnston, S. (2010). Rita, Sue and Andrea Too. *The Daily Telegraph.* 16/10/10

Lister, D.A.J. (2004). *Bradford's Own.* The History Press.

McCormick, F. (1989). Where the Heart is. *Yorkshire Post.* 28/1/89.

Rita, Sue and Bob Too. (1987). [film]. UK: Alan Clarke.

Shepherd, R. (1987). The Talk of the Town. *Sunday Times Magazine*. 6/9/1987.

Telegraph & Argus. (1987). Berlin Praises Local Film. 6/7/87.

Telegraph & Argus. (1989). Sequel on the way. 21/12/89.

Telegraph & Argus. (1990). She Collapses in Pub, Aged 29. 21/12/90.

Telegraph & Argus. (1989). More Barrels of Dunbar Fun. 2/12/89.

Yorkshire Post. (1990). Last Tributes for Playwright. 29/12/90.

1: Hard Scratch

Arena: Andrea Dunbar & Victoria Wood. (1980). [TV programme] BBC2: BBC. 26/3/80.

Barrett-Lee, L., & Shaw, J. (2014). *My Mam Shirley: Tales of the Notorious Hudson Family – Canterbury Warriors Book 3*. Harper Collins.

Birdsall, M. & Szekely, G. & Walker, P. (2002). *The Illustrated History of Bradford's Suburbs*. Breedon Books Publishing Co Ltd.

Bradford Council. (1991). *The GBH Report: An Integrated Comprehensive Regeneration Strategy for Buttershaw*. Bradford: Bradford Council.

Dunbar, A. (1988*). Rita, Sue and Bob Too with The Arbor and*

Shirley; Three stage plays by Andrea Dunbar. Methuen New Theatrescript.

Gardner, L. (1998). Born to Write and Die. *The Guardian*. 04/07/98.

The Great North Show: In Praise of Bad Girls. (1989). [TV programme]. Yorkshire TV. 31/01/89.

Greenhalf, J. (1987). Face to Face with Andrea Dunbar. *Telegraph & Argus*. 18/8/1987.

Greenhalf, J. (2003). *It's a Mean Old Scene: A History of Modern Bradford from 1974*. Redbeck Press.

Hargreaves, J.A. (2004). Dunbar, Andrea (1961–1990). *Oxford Dictionary of National Biography*. Oxford University Press.

Pearce, L. (2016). *Private Collection of Dunbar Family*. Letters and Documents.

Remembering Andrea Dunbar. (2010). [TV Programme]. Inside Out. BBC One. 23/10/10.

Shepherd, R. (1987). The Talk of the Town. *Sunday Times Magazine*, p. 32. 06/09/87.

Some Case Studies from Buttershaw. (1974). Bradford.

Sunset Boulevard: A Study of Housing Conditions in Buttershaw. (1975). Bradford.

Telegraph & Argus. (1980). A Divided Community. 01/04/80.

Veitch, A. (1980). Getting out of Buttershaw. *The Guardian*. 21/03/80.

2: Paper Sheets

The Arbor. (2010). [film]. UK: Clio Barnard.

Bellerby, R. (2005). *Chasing the Sixpence; The Lives of Bradford Mill Folk.* Fort Publishing.

Dunbar, A. (1988*). Rita, Sue and Bob Too with The Arbor and Shirley; Three stage plays by Andrea Dunbar.* Methuen New Theatrescript.

Goodhart, D. (2011). A Tale of Three Cities. Prospect Magazine.

Greenhalf, J. (2003). *It's a Mean Old Scene: A History of Modern Bradford from 1974.* Redbeck Press.

Hargreaves, J.A. (2004). Dunbar, Andrea (1961-1990). *Oxford Dictionary of National Biography.* Oxford University Press.

Joseph Rowntree Foundation. (2005). *Researching Bradford; A review of social research on Bradford District.*

Keighley, M. (2007). *Wool City: A history of the Bradford textile industry in the 20th century.* G. Whitaker & Co.

Lister, D.A.J. (2004). *Bradford's Own.* The History Press.

Soans, R. (2000). Drugs, poverty . . . at least no one's nicked the postbox 'Rita, Sue and Bob Too' captured life on a council estate in Thatcher's Britain. Almost 20 years later, where would its update find inspiration? *The Independent.*

3: The Next One Could Be Innocent

The Arbor. (2010). [film] UK: Clio Barnard.

Armstrong, S. (2013). *The Road to Wigan Pier Revisited.* Constable.

Bilton, M. (2006). *Wicked Beyond Belief: The Hunt for the Yorkshire Ripper.* Harper Perennial.

Dunbar, A. (1988*). Rita, Sue and Bob Too with The Arbor and Shirley; Three stage plays by Andrea Dunbar.* Methuen New Theatrescript.

Nicholson, M. (1979). *The Yorkshire Ripper: A Factual Account.* Star.

The Great North Show: In Praise of Bad Girls. (1989). [TV programme]. Yorkshire TV.

Ward Jouve, N. (1986). *The Streetcleaner: The Yorkshire Ripper Case on Trial.* Marion Boyars.

4: Red Mist

Brown, J. (2001). *The Oxford Illustrated History of Theatre.* New York: Oxford University Press. p.428

Dunbar, A. (1988*). Rita, Sue and Bob Too with The Arbor and Shirley; Three stage plays by Andrea Dunbar.* Methuen New Theatrescript.

Lewenstein, O. (1994). *Kicking Against the Pricks: A Theatre Producer Looks Back.* London: Nick Hern Books.

Pearce, J. and Milne, E. (2010). *Participation and community*

on Bradford's traditionally white estates. Joseph Rowntree
Foundation.

Pearce, L. (2016). *Private Collection of Dunbar Family.*
Letters and Documents.

Rita, Sue and Bob Too. (1987). [film]. UK: Alan Clarke.

Roberts, P., Stafford-Clark, M. and Haynes, J. (2007).
Taking Stock. London: Nick Hern Books Ltd.

Roberts. P. (1999). *The Royal Court and the Modern Stage
(Cambridge Studies in Modern Theatre).* Cambridge
University Press.

Royal Court Theatre, (2015). *History.* [online] Available at:
http://www.royalcourttheatre.com/ [Accessed 1 Sep.
2015].

Stafford-Clark, M. (2008). *The Legacy of the English Stage
Company.* [Audio Recording]. British Library Sound
Archive.

Wainwright, M. (1994). Stress, kids and cigs. *The Guardian.*

5: Muck or Nettles

Arena: Andrea Dunbar & Victoria Wood. (1980). [TV
programme] BBC2: BBC. 26/3/80.

Aston, E. & Reinelt, J. (2001). Building Bridges: Life on
Dunbar's Arbor, Past and Present. *Theatre Research
International.* Vol. 26 (03). 10/01.

Cadwallader, A. (1980). Misery play catapults Andrea to
fame. *The Times.* 26/3/80.

Dorney, K. (2013). *Played in Britain*. London: Bloomsbury Publishing.

Gardner, L. (1998). Born to Write and Die. *The Guardian*. 04/07/98.

Gardner, L. (2000). 'The middle classes are the movers and shakers. They get things done'. *The Guardian*. 15/11/00.

The Great North Show: In Praise of Bad Girls. (1989). [TV programme]. Yorkshire TV. 31/01/89.

Johnston, S. (2010). Rita, Sue and Andrea Too. *The Daily Telegraph*. 16/10/10.

Keighley News. (1980). First Play Brings Acclaim. 28/03/80.

Limmer, K. (2003). Investigating the Authority of the Literary Text in Critical Debate. *Forum Media 6 Journal*. Issue 5. The Polytechnic Institute of Viseu, Portugal.

Ritchie, R. (1988). *Rita, Sue and Bob Too* with *The Arbor* and *Shirley*. Introduction. Methuen Drama.

Roberts. P. (1999). *The Royal Court and the Modern Stage (Cambridge Studies in Modern Theatre)*. Cambridge University Press.

Russell, D. (2004). *Looking North: Northern England and the National Imagination*. Manchester University Press.

Soans, R. (2000). *A State Affair*. Methuen Drama.

Stafford-Clark, M. (2000). How's it been for Rita, Sue and Bob Too? *The Sunday Times*. 15/10/00.

Stafford-Clark, M. (2008). *The Legacy of the English Stage Company*. [Audio Recording]. British Library Sound Archive.

Roberts. P. & Stafford-Clark, M. (2007) *Taking Stock; The Theatre of Max Stafford-Clark*. Nick Hern Books.

The Times. (1980). Royal Court to Show Play by Girl Aged 18. 4/06/80.

Tirbutt, S. (1987). Nasty, Brutish Bradford Life. *Telegraph & Argus*.15/3/80.

Veitch, A. (1980). Getting out of Buttershaw. *The Guardian*. 21/03/80.

Wardle, I. (1981). Why the Royal Court must prevail. *The Times*. 21/09/81.

6: Two Nations

The Arbor. (2010). [film] UK: Clio Barnard.

Aston, E. & Reinelt, J. (2001). Building Bridges: Life on Dunbar's Arbor, Past and Present. *Theatre Research International*. Vol. 26 (03). 10/01.

Billington, M. (1986). Shirley. *The Guardian*. 1/05/86

Burn, G. (1984). *Somebody's Husband, Somebody's Son: The Story of the Yorkshire Ripper*. Heinemann.

Cooper, N. (2002). Rita, Sue and a true story, too. *The Herald*. Glasgow. 12/02/02.

The Daily Mail. (1982). Price of a Ripper Victim's Anguish. 19/04/82.

Dunbar, A. (1988*). Rita, Sue and Bob Too with The Arbor and Shirley; Three stage plays by Andrea Dunbar*. Methuen New Theatrescript.

Dunbar, A. & Stafford-Clark, M. (1981-85). Letters and Correspondence. Royal Court Archive, V&A Blyth House, London.

Gardner, L. (1998). Born to Write and Die. *The Guardian.* 04/07/98.

The Great North Show: In Praise of Bad Girls. (1989). [TV programme]. Yorkshire TV. 31/01/89.

Greenhalf, J. (2003). *It's a Mean Old Scene: A History of Modern Bradford from 1974.* Redbeck Press.

Oscar Lewenstein Production Papers. (1952-1974). V&A Theatre and Performance Archive.

Limmer, K. (2003). Investigating the Authority of the Literary Text in Critical Debate. *Forum Media 6 Journal.* Issue 5. The Polytechnic Institute of Viseu, Portugal.

Moore, O. (1982). Young Writers' Festival. *Evening Standard.* 10/82.

Nightingale, B. (1982). *New Statesman.* 29/10/82.

Ritchie, R. (1988). *Rita, Sue and Bob Too* with *The Arbor* and *Shirley.* Introduction. Methuen Drama.

Roberts. P. & Stafford-Clark, M. (2007) *Taking Stock; The Theatre of Max Stafford-Clark.* Nick Hern Books.

Shepherd, R. (1987). The Talk of the Town. *Sunday Times Magazine.* 6/9/1987.

Soans, R. (2000). *A State Affair.* Methuen Drama.

Stafford-Clark, M. (2000). *Rita, Sue and Bob Too / A State Affair (foreword).* Methuen Drama.

Stafford-Clark, M. (2008). *The Legacy of the English Stage*

Company. [Audio Recording]. British Library Sound
Archive.

7: Shooting the Messenger

The Arbor. (2010). [film] UK: Clio Barnard.

Behrens, D. (1998). No Hard Feelings Andrea. *Telegraph &
Argus*. 15/06/98.

Cooper, N. (2002). Rita, Sue and a true story, too. *The
Herald*. Glasgow. 12/02/02.

Dunbar, A. (1987*)*. Column. *Yorkshire Post*. 6/6/87.

Dunbar, A. (1988*)*. *Rita, Sue and Bob Too with The Arbor and
Shirley; Three stage plays by Andrea Dunbar*. Methuen New
Theatrescript.

Earnshaw, T. & Moran, J. (2008). *Made in Yorkshire*.
Guerilla Books.

El-Khairy, O. (2011). Clio Barnard's Talking Heads. *Mute*.
Vol. 3 (1).

Film Four International. (1987). *Rita, Sue and Bob Too!*

Gardner, L. (1998). Born to Write and Die. *The Guardian*.
04/07/98.

Garford, A. (1987:13).'Life's not like that around here'.
Telegraph & Argus. 29/05/87

The Great North Show: In Praise of Bad Girls. (1989). [TV
programme]. Yorkshire TV. 31/01/89.

Greenhalf, J. (1987). Face to Face with Andrea Dunbar.
Telegraph & Argus. 18/8/1987.

Greenhalf, J. (2003). *It's a Mean Old Scene: A History of Modern Bradford from 1974*. Redbeck Press.

Hargreaves, J.A. (2004). Dunbar, Andrea (1961-1990). *Oxford Dictionary of National Biography*. Oxford University Press.

Harper, S. (2000). *Women in British Cinema: Mad, Bad and Dangerous to Know*. Continuum.

Holdsworth, P. (1987). Rita, Sue and Bob Too. *Telegraph & Argus*. 08/09/87.

Holdsworth, P. (1991). Compassion Behind the Bluntness. *Telegraph & Argus*. 5/1/91.

Holdsworth, P. (1991). *Andrea Dunbar, A Tribute*. Telegraph & Argus / Bradford Libraries and Information Service.

Hobday, J. (2016). *BFI Screenonline: 'One of Thatcher's Children'. Screenonline.org.uk*. Retrieved 6 March 2016, from http://www.screenonline.org.uk/tv/id/445090/index.html

Hutchinson, T. (1987). *Lust for Life in Slumland*. Mail on Sunday. 04/09/87.

Johnston, S. (2010). Rita, Sue and Andrea Too. *The Daily Telegraph*. 16/10/10.

Kelly, J. (1987:25). *Genius Straight from the Slums*. Mail on Sunday. 26/07/87.

Kelly, R. (1998). *Alan Clarke*. Faber and Faber.

Limmer, K. (2003). Investigating the Authority of the Literary Text in Critical Debate. *Forum Media 6 Journal*. Issue 5. The Polytechnic Institute of Viseu, Portugal.

Lister, D.A.J. (2004). *Bradford's Own*. The History Press.

Malcolm, D. (1987). Nowt but truth. *The Guardian*. 03/09/87.

Mantel, H. (1987). Bonkers in Bradford. *The Spectator*. 18/09/87.

New Musical Express. (1987). Frozen Sausage Frenzy. 06/09/87.

O'Sullivan, S. (2006). No Such thing as Society: Television and the Apocalypse. In: L. Friedman, ed. *Fires Were Started: British Cinema and Thatcherism*. Wallflower Press.

Pearce, G. (1987). The film that turned the festival blue. *Daily Express*. 25/05/87.

Rita, Sue and Bob Too. (1987). [film]. UK: Alan Clarke.

Ritchie, R. (1988). *Rita, Sue and Bob Too* with *The Arbor* and *Shirley*. Introduction. Methuen Drama.

Roberts, E. (1998). Buttershaw Revisited. *Yorkshire Post*. 01/06/98.

Roberts. P. & Stafford-Clark, M. (2007) *Taking Stock; The Theatre of Max Stafford-Clark*. Nick Hern Books.

Rolinson, D. (2005). Television Series: Alan Clarke, *Form and Narrative in the 1980s*, Manchester University Press.

Russell, D. (2003). Selling Bradford, Tourism and Northern Image in the Late Twentieth Century. *Contemporary British History*. Vol. 19 (1). University of Central Lancashire.

Screen International. (1986). Rita, Sue and Bob Too. Issue 561.16/08/86.

Shepherd, R. (1987). The Talk of the Town. *Sunday Times Magazine*. 6/9/1987.

Stafford-Clark, M. (2008). *The Legacy of the English Stage Company*. [Audio Recording]. British Library Sound Archive.

The Sunday Times. (1987). Cannes Openers. 12/04/87.

Telegraph & Argus. (1987). Crowds Rush to Rita, Sue and Bob Too. 24/9/87.

Telegraph & Argus. (1987). Berlin Praises Local Film. 6/7/87.

Telegraph & Argus. (1987). Film Knocks City's Image. 25/05/87.

Telegraph & Argus. (1987). Stars defend 'offensive' film. 26/05/87

Yorkshire Evening Post. (1986). Cameras Roll on Andrea's Epic. 28/8/86.

Yorkshire Post. (1987). Estates of the Nation. 9/9/87.

8: Last Orders

Ackroyd, R. (1988). Court Report. *Telegraph & Argus*. 15/12/88.

The Arbor. (2010). [film] UK: Clio Barnard.

Gardner, L. (1998). Born to Write and Die. *The Guardian*. 04/07/98.

The Great North Show: In Praise of Bad Girls. (1989). [TV programme]. Yorkshire TV. 31/01/89.

Johnston, S. (2010). Rita, Sue and Andrea Too. *The Daily Telegraph.* 16/10/10.

Kay Mellor. (2015). *BFI.* Retrieved 23 March 2016, from http://www.bfi.org.uk/films-tv-people/4ce2ba840467a

McCormick, F. (1989). Where the Heart is. *Yorkshire Post.* 28/1/89.

Mellor, K. (2010). Award-winning playwright Kay Mellor believed her mother had always been faithful to her father. Then a tear-racked confession changed everything. *Daily Mail.* 09/04/2010

Roberts. P. & Stafford-Clark, M. (2007) *Taking Stock; The Theatre of Max Stafford-Clark.* Nick Hern Books.

Stafford-Clark, M. (2008). *The Legacy of the English Stage Company.* [Audio Recording]. British Library Sound Archive.

Telegraph & Argus. (1989). Why our Andrea is Happy to Bide her Time. 31/1/89.

Acknowledgements

The Society of Authors' 2016 K Blundell Trust Award for Fiction helped me to complete this novel, thanks to all involved and the Authors' Foundation for their assistance.

For their support and input I would like to thank: Russ Litten and Shane Rhodes at Wrecking Ball Press for their encouragement and belief that this story needed to be told, Gill Armstrong for her eagle-eye and all of those who read various drafts – Jenni Fagan, Amy Liptrot, Darran Anderson, Zaffar Kunial, Kester Aspden and Richard Benson. My fantastic agent Matthew Hamilton at Aitken Alexander. Ursula Doyle and all at Fleet. Jeff Barrett & Diva Harris. Lee Brackstone. Paul Baggaley. The Dunbar sisters: Jeanette, Kathy, and Pamela. The ever-enthusiastic Lisa Pearce, thank you for making me laugh and sharing your memories of Andrea.

I would like to express my deepest gratitude to Paul Ward, Michael Stewart, Simon Crump, Sarah Falcus, and David

Rudrum at the University of Huddersfield. Katy Shaw at Leeds Beckett. Jalna Hanmer. Liane Aukin for her wise words and black wit. Max Stafford-Clark, Carole Hayman and Rob Ritchie. Abby Dix-Mason and Matthew Davison. Paul Barber, Siobhan Finneran, George Costigan, Ed Tudor-Pole and Janet Horsfield. Heidi James. Jane Kelly. Jim Greenhalf. Carol Gorner. Claire Malcolm at New Writing North and Chris Taylor. Andy Brydon for keeping me alive in the winter months. Kay Mellor. Ken Loach. Dene Michael (Black Lace). Chloé Raunet and Ivan Smagghe. Emma and Tim Stripe. Pam Hall.

Bradford Local Studies Library, Bradford Industrial Museum, BFI Special Collections, British Library Reading Rooms at Boston Spa, Leeds Central Library, Royal Court Archive at the V&A, and the West Yorkshire Archive Service.

I would particularly like to thank Claire MacDonald for her generosity and Lisa Cradduck for her friendship and invaluable advice on working-class culture.

To my sister Katy, and father, Ian – without you I'd be lost. Had my mother lived to see the publication of this book I'm sure she would have been delighted to read it. Thank you Mum, for always being there.

A final, special mention to my husband Benjamin Myers, who has endured over four years of conversations about Andrea Dunbar and everything connected to the subject. Without his love and support *Black Teeth and a Brilliant Smile* would not have been written. This book is for him.

FLEET

To buy any of our books and to find out
more about Fleet, our authors and titles, as well
as events and book clubs, visit our website

www.littlebrown.co.uk

and follow us on Twitter

**@FleetReads
@LittleBrownUK**

To order any Fleet titles p & p free in the UK,
please contact our mail order supplier on:

+ 44 (0)1832 737525

Customers not based in the UK should contact
the same number for appropriate postage
and packing costs.